CRAVING HIS MATE

FATED MATES OF THE ATARI

A. G. WILDE

PETRONIE PUBLISHING

CRAVING HIS MATE

From the moment my fangs began to drip with life spirit, I have known I wanted a mate. One to love. One to care for. _A female that will be mine._

But as the moons pass by, the fates have denied me.

Until I see her.

She is different. She is human. _And she is vulnerable._ More vulnerable than I could have ever imagined.

But she is _mine_. Mine to cherish, mine to keep, and I will do everything in my power to let her know that the moment I laid my eyes on her, she became the reason I breathe.

BEFORE YOU READ!

This book touches on some dark themes, including murder, death, and abuse of a differently-abled person.
If any of this is something that will negatively affect your reading experience, please stop here. I understand if you'd rather skip this book.
No worries! I have many other books I'm sure you would enjoy.
If you choose to read on, enjoy!

 AG

1

Trudy

It's dark down here, but I must have gotten used to the lack of light because I have no trouble seeing the vermin approaching. Eyes so black they blend in with the darkness around us, the alien coming toward me uses his whip against the back of the poor soul crouched before him.

The whip cracks, shattering the heavy air, followed by the cry of the slave at the alien's feet.

Big, tall, scaly...these captors all look the same. Same species with sharp, jagged teeth and hairless scaly bodies. Skin that looks like a sickly dark gray, or maybe blue...I can't tell in this light. Or maybe I don't know because I never stare at them for too long. They walk with those whips and don't hesitate to use them in this cavern where we have nowhere to run.

Not that I *could* run...even though I want to.

Shifting, I turn my gaze to the rock wall before me, my fingers shivering as I grip my pick and continue working away at the hard stone.

Look busy. Find those green gems they want. Ensure your safety.

It's the only way to keep alive.

As the captor moves down the line, some of the other aliens mining the gems whimper. I try not to, but my shoulders still stiffen, the skin at the back of my neck prickling, the hairs standing on end.

That unease rides like a wave down the rest of my body and I force my breaths to steady. I grip the pick and I slam it into the rock before me. It latches, and I have to pull hard to get it out, only to slam it into the wall again. Dust and small shards of rock break away as I work.

Held tight between my thighs is the little bucket that will hold my gems. I need to find at least one before my shift ends, or I'll get no food. Worse. I'll be punished. Whipped…or even worse than that.

The platform we sit on shakes as the captor nears. It's taken a long time for me to get used to the sway whenever someone moves, and I force myself not to look behind me. To keep my eyes from venturing to the frail barrier that lines the platform's edge—the only thing protecting us from what looks like certain death beyond. For behind me is an abyss. A hole to hell. As far as I know, there is no end to it…and I have seen these bitches throw people over the railing before. Once when some poor slave stood up to them. Another time when an elderly female failed to find gems three times in a row.

I can still hear her cry fade as she fell into the hole. I didn't hear her land. Her cry just faded into nothing. For all I know, this mine shaft, the hole behind me, leads to the center of this planet.

So as the captor comes closer, I work my pick like the good little miner that I am.

How long has it been since they threw me into this cold cavern? I'm not sure. Days blend into one another when there is no light from the sun. But the circumstances that got me here seem far away.

That ship I was on. The luxury cruise my government had organized. The one I took only because it was free…all that seems like so long ago. My one chance at space travel had turned into an ongoing nightmare.

The only thing that feels fresh is the memory of all those women who died on that ship after it was seized. I keep seeing them being cut down before me. I hear their cries in my sleep. I feel the warmth of their blood as if it was still splashing against me.

I don't know *why* I survived. I don't know why those brutes that took our ship kept me alive and brought me here to this place.

"*You,*" the captor stops behind me and I freeze, my thoughts glitching and dissolving to the back of my mind. He's right behind me.

Shit. Not me. Don't look at me.

But when his claws grip the shoulder of the poor alien beside me, a breath shudders from my body, followed closely by a sense of guilt. Humanoid with pale blue skin, the alien male who was working by my side shakes so hard his pick falls from his fingers. I don't want to be in his position. I don't want the captor to target me; yet, as he pulls the blue alien away and forces him to continue down the winding platform, relief mixes in with the guilt.

I watch as he takes him so far, they disappear, leaving the station next to me wide open.

I swallow hard, ignoring the wariness crawling up my spine.

That blue alien had been fine. Good. Trustworthy enough to not try to rob me of my gems. The one to my right, not so much. Skin green like the envy that lurks in his gaze, the male on my right has had his eyes on my bucket more than once. Each day, I get the feeling he's only being civil because he's managed to find gems as well. Who knows what sort of creature they will put in the now vacant place by my side.

The platform shakes again as another one of the scaly captors approaches.

Two of them? My pick stalls in my hand, every instinct inside me going haywire. In my time here, I've never seen two of these scaly beings in the same spot on the platform at once. Why now? What's happening?

"This one? This small female?" he growls in Galactic Standard, glancing upward to another of his kind above. My heart wallops and falls like stone. I've long since learned that being singled out in this mine is one of the worst things that could ever happen to any of us slaves.

But as I hazard a glance behind me, I realize he's pointing to an alien two places over. He isn't referring to me. I swallow hard, trying to calm my nerves as I grip the pick in my hand. The alien is small and delicate. Like a forest nymph, she stands out in this place filled with dark stone. I can see the fear vibrating through her and the captor's nostrils flare as if he can smell it.

From somewhere above us, his colleague shouts the affirmative. "Yes, take that one. She found no gems last cycle."

My throat goes dry, my heart still that heavy boulder in my chest as the captor grips the female's arm and pulls her away.

My gaze drops to my bucket.

I found two gems yesterday. Small ones, about the size of the nail on my little finger, but enough to appease our captors. I remember the forest nymph's whimper when our shifts were over and she had yet to find any gems.

I'd offered her one of mine, and her terrified wide eyes had only stared at me as if she thought I was playing some trick on her.

The green male beside me growls softly. "You're the one they should have taken. You are at a disadvantage here...yet you find gems every day."

My jaw clenches and I refuse to give him the pleasure of my gaze. "I'm disabled," I snap under my breath. "Not dead."

Tilting my head as covertly as I can, I watch our captors pull the small nymph away. The platform shakes with their departure, and I wonder just what fate these evils have in store for her.

It is only when the hairs at the back of my neck stand on end that I realize the other captor, the one who had taken the blue alien below, has returned to stand behind me.

"You too," he says, his Galactic Standard coming out rough and unfriendly.

I freeze.

He's not talking to me, right?

But something makes me glance over my shoulder and I find those soulless eyes on me.

"Follow me," he snarls, not waiting for even a second before he continues along the platform.

I stare in his wake. Fear, uncertainty, panic, and anxiety all crawling up my spine and filling my gut.

"You had better make haste," the green male to my right says. "You don't want to anger the Morang. They are not known for their patience."

He stares right at me, a small sneer on his lips, obviously relieved I'm the one that's been singled out and not him. But, even though I don't like him, I know his words are true.

"But..." My words evaporate from my lips, forming condensation in this cold cavern. "But I find gems every day!" I say louder, loud enough for the Morang walking away from me to hear.

He pauses and the air feels chilled even more than it already is.

For a moment, I wonder why I am soaking in stupidity. Why I am bargaining to remain in this place rather than follow my captors wherever they are taking me?

Because you know that it's nowhere good, Trudz. No female that they take from the mines ever returns and you know they don't set them free.

Beings like this won't just set you free.

When the Morang turns and his gaze settles on me, I feel my mortality for a moment. If he wants to throw me off this platform into that abyss, he can. If he wants to use his sharp teeth to rip into me, he can. I have no power here.

"Move!" he roars, and my pick falls from my hand.

Swallowing hard, I nod immediately, using my hands to pull my legs from underneath me where I've been resting on them.

They feel like ice, but I ignore it, even as tears prick into my eyes.

I can do this. I can...

As I crawl toward him, pulling my limp legs behind me, I refuse to let the tears filling my eyes to escape down my cheeks. It's not the first time I've had to crawl. My legs may not work, but my hands do. I don't need anyone's pity. I can—

The Morang growls again and releases a sound in his throat just as I reach his feet. "Pitiful," he says before turning and continuing up the winding platform.

I swallow down my fear and follow.

It's hard.

My legs might feel like ice, but my fingers do too.

The pieces of cloth I'd torn from my blouse to wrap and protect my hands are almost completely stripped away and the callouses on my palm hurt as I pull myself along.

But what's really hard is the eyes on my back.

I can feel them looking—all the other slaves that I pass. I can feel their discomfort, some of their relief that they're not the ones targeted, and their pity. For a moment, I look up at the back of the Morang, who's now several feet ahead of me, and pure thick hatred fills my soul.

I'd had a wheelchair that their comrades had crushed after they'd pulled me from it. That chair was my legs. The only way I traveled around on Lower Earth.

Sniffing, I continue on, my head lifting as I look up at the winding platform. Only the dim torches line the wall that leads to the top of the cavern, and I see no light of day.

Bits of rock shards that fell on the platform dig into my arms and my skin, but I continue anyway. I tell myself it will be over soon. This is just a moment in eternity.

I can survive this.

I *will* survive this.

When the Morang suddenly stops at one of the small offshoots that branch from the main shaft, I release a slow breath. Those offshoots are where we rest when not working. He's only repositioning me.

But his words send a chill down my spine.

"—must take this one to the boss as well."

A Morang pops his head out, his grasp on the nymph-like alien causing her to be pulled forward as well. His gaze locks on me at the same time that her wide eyes do.

"That female is broken..."

"But enough to harden a soft cock. Bring her. Females are scarce in these mines. He won't be expecting much."

2

Qhenno

Finding the humans has been more difficult than I expected. Luckily, Aqnar, second in command of our expedition, has already found one. The other three that survived the attack on their ship, however, have found no such luck.

Frowning at the schematics in front of me, I tick off every station that we have checked, a low growl of annoyance leaving my throat.

Bhihan, third in command and the only other person on this vessel with me, walks in, his entrance making the air around me shift.

I growl again.

"Don't growl at me as if I am your mate," he says, plopping into the seat in front of me. In his hand is a receptacle filled with *floosh* jelly, an icy sweet varnish that is usually not eaten on its own.

I frown at him, my annoyance growing. "How can you sit there all unconcerned eating *floosh*? Three females are unaccounted for."

"And they're probably dead," he says, leveling his gaze with mine. "A whole moon has passed and still no sign of them." He squeezes some floosh into his mouth, his disregard making my nostrils flare.

"You're so invested…it's as if you and Da'red believe you will find your mates if you look hard enough."

The back of my neck tightens, and I have to remind myself that Bhihan is my friend, my *ally*, not my enemy. But his words…they make some kind of beast roil deep within me.

"Aqnar was lucky," he continues. "He found one of the females. She turned out to be his mate." He levels his gaze with mine again, taking his time to squeeze some more floosh into his mouth. I have never seen a more annoying gesture until this moment. "There are thousands of Atari males like you and me. Come back to reality, Qhenno. Not all of us will find mates…much less with three random Earthkin females. Chances are, you might find one of these females and she turns out to be the mate of some Atari back on homeworld."

I don't hold back the growl that swells in my chest, and Bhihan lifts an eyebrow at me.

"Not everyone is like you, Bhihan. Not all of us have accepted that we might be mateless." I turn my gaze back to the schematic. "Some of us will do everything to find those females, even if they turn out to be someone else's mate."

Because a mate is precious. I would do anything to find one for myself. And if it was my mate lost out there somewhere, I would hope some Atari warrior would do everything to keep her safe until I could.

Bhihan releases a sigh, but I don't look at him again.

He may pretend he doesn't care about these females, but I have seen the schematics he has taken back to his quarters. I have seen the communication logs. The calls to unknown stations in the outer reaches that *he* made. He is just as worried about these females as I am. For some stupid reason I don't have the time to scrutinize, he is pretending as if he doesn't.

"Your stubbornness concerning this is baffling," I murmur, frowning as I go over the schematic for the fifth yora in a row. I must have missed a station somewhere. One that could give us a lead.

"Not all of us will find a mate, Qhenno," he repeats. "It's simple logic."

My eyes dart to him but my retort is interrupted by a sudden buzz in the ship.

"Must be Da'red contacting us to update his location again." Bhihan is about to rise to accept the communication but I beat him to it.

"Zarzenius command," I answer the call with the name of our mothership.

"Qhenno, I have word." I frown for a second when it is not the voice of our prince on the line. "Dred?"

"Aye...I, uh, I think I found one of your hoogmans," Dred says. For a bounty hunter, one would think he'd take more care in learning the name of the species he's paid to look out for.

"*Humans*, you *snizz*," Bhihan hisses. I ignore him, but he's forgotten the floosh on the side of the control panel and is now right beside me, breathing over my back as if he wasn't just telling me to forget about the humans.

I shoot an annoyed glance over my shoulder, meeting his golden gaze with a glare.

"Where did you find her?" I press.

"I didn't. Only glimpsed a female of the description you gave," Dred says. "Small. Mostly hairless. Like a pale, little version of an Atari female."

"*Where?*" He's taking too long to give the information, and that is never a good sign. Unease creeps into the sensitive skin at the back of my neck, and I rub a hand over it to ease the tension. "Can you take guardianship of her? We can jump to your location and collect her. Just let us—"

"Not going near where she is with a three-footed carcep," Dred says. "She's in Morang territory."

Silence descends on the ship as if even the automated controls have forgotten how to beep.

"No," I whisper.

"Qef," Bhihan mutters, finally moving from over my shoulder to pace behind me.

"You can't mean..." The words trail from my lips to end in silence.

"Yes. Working in one of those mines. Near impossible for you to get her out of there unless you have some Karmachi gems in your posses-sion..." Dred pauses as if waiting for an answer and something heavy falls in my chest.

"Of course, we don't have Karmachi gems. Only the Morang have that currency. They do not trade Karmachi with other species. They are *obsessed* with it."

Dred grunts. "Like the Atari are obsessed with Arzentus?"

He has a point. Arzentus, or "gold" as the humans call it, is the metal we traded with New Earth for. It's the reason we're searching for these females. They were part of the deal, given to us by their world as part of the trade. A bridal gift. In all senses of the word, all females that were on that doomed vessel are now Atari. And we never leave our people behind. Especially precious females.

But some of what Dred said makes little sense. "If she is in one of those mines, how did *you* find her? No one enters those mines and escapes unharmed."

Dred makes a sound as if he is disagreeing. "Saw her in a Morang tavern. The Morang boss had his slaves on display. No idea how long she'll be there for…if she survives."

My skin bristles. He means…if she survives the Morang.

"Send me the coordinates," I say, already walking toward the shuttle bay.

"What?" Bhihan is at my back. "You can't go to Morang territory. You will have no protection there. They do not recognize Atar as allies and their network is outside our reach."

"I know," I reply, not slowing down.

"Then why are you still walking?"

When I don't stop, Bhihan releases a growl of frustration, his fist closing over my shoulder, stopping my forward movement.

"Qhenno, you are the helmsman of this ship. Zarzenius needs you. *I* will go."

For a moment, I am surprised by his offer. So I was right about him caring about these females.

I grasp his fist on my shoulder, squeezing it lightly.

I have fought many battles with this male. The males who traveled with me on this ship have become as close to me as my own kin. But that won't stop me from going after this female.

"I will go," I say and Bhihan's expression morphs into anger.

"First you say I do not care, now you will not let me go in your stead. Do you have a motling nesting in your ears? I said the Zarzenius needs you."

"You can fly the ship as well as I can," I reply, grabbing supplies from the storage shelves as I continue toward the shuttle bay. "But that's not the only reason I won't let you go."

Bhihan stops, mild confusion flooding his gaze. "What do you mean?"

"I don't know, Bhihan." I turn as I step through the doors that mark the entrance to the bay, turning to face him when I am on the other side. "I just know that *I* have to go."

He releases a breath before suddenly slamming a fist into the wall at his side. "Qef the fates, don't tell me you're feeling a call."

I stare at him as the doors close, watching his mouth move as he curses some more.

Thing is, I don't know if it's a call. After all, I've never felt the call of the fates before.

All I know is that I need to go save this female.

No matter what it takes, I must find her…

Whoever she is.

3

Trudy

Glancing around the busy interior of the club, I know there has to be a way out of this.

I'm not in that dark mine shaft anymore. I'm somewhere above ground and if there's an entrance to this place, it means there's an exit, too.

It's been three days since they took us from the depths of the mine.

And for three days, I have tried to find a way out. I'm not giving up until I do.

Sitting upright, I take only a quick breath before continuing to pull myself across the floor, one arm leading the way and pulling me forward while I balance a tray with two drinks in the other.

I move slowly, trying to keep myself going and the drinks stable. The last thing I want is for someone to bump into me, or for me to lose my balance and spill the beverages.

It's happened twice before, and both times I could feel the gaze of the head Morang on my back, even in a place crowded like this.

The crowd dips and sways, making it hard to move around when

I'm on the floor, dodging feet and tails. But even though the crowd is such a hindrance, it's also my best bet at getting out of here.

Maybe I can get lost in it. Slink away while these brutes dance and enjoy themselves. If these drinks I'm having to serve will get them drunk, even the better. I just have to find the exit and slip away and then…

And then I find a way off this rock.

I just have to get out of here first.

Head turned in the direction I'm going, the crowd parts for a moment and my gaze lands on the boss. A shiver goes down my spine when I find those soulless eyes locked on me. He's the biggest of all the brutes in this place. I can sense the negative energy wafting off him like a thick perfume.

Swallowing hard, I try to calm my nerves as I continue moving across the dance floor.

I don't understand why he's kept me here after seeing that I can't walk. The implication makes a sour patch develop in my throat, one that I can't swallow away.

Back on Lower Earth, males like him exist by the dozen. Males who don't mind taking advantage of vulnerable females like me.

I shudder again at the thought.

He hasn't killed me…yet. I have to focus on that, because if I don't, I'll spiral and the fear crawling along my spine will have me for dinner.

I find his gems. Despite my legs, I am good at finding those blasted green gems because I don't stop digging until I do.

It's the only way to survive. *And I will survive this.* So maybe… maybe that's why he hasn't killed me yet. Why he has me serving him drinks. Why he hasn't stopped me from doing the most inefficient task I could have possibly received in this hyped-up tavern.

Continuing to pull myself along the floor, my palm aches every time I have to put all my weight on it, but I am careful to keep my face as blank as I can. When someone almost stumbles over me, a surprised exclamation then a curse coming from their lips, I don't even look up. I push away the shame that threatens to cascade over me.

I should have artificial limbs, implants—or, at the very least, *my chair.* But those things on Lower Earth are scarce. Good ones, at least.

Ones that won't cost you a year's worth of rations, plus the arm and leg you're trying to save. I'm just lucky this section of the club isn't as busy as the other side. Fewer people to bump into. I can only assume that the boss-reptilian guy is the reason.

Even his own people seem afraid of him.

As I pull myself, the elbow that presses into the cold floor burns with the effort to balance me and the tray on top of it, but I go the last few feet until I finally see the dark clawed toes of the Morang boss before me.

I pause, forcing myself to release a slow breath instead of the heavy pants that want to leave my chest.

"Your...highness?" I say, uncertainty threading into the edge of my voice as I dip my head, my gaze on his feet as I lift the tray higher.

"How *curious*..." he says. Those are words that hold no threat...yet, the snarl underneath his voice makes me shiver. His feet shift as if he has leaned forward, but I do not lift my gaze to his. He'll only see the bitterness in my eyes. The hatred for him and this place. So I keep my gaze on his feet, and feel disgust instead. "A unique little asset," he continues. "The strange female of a species I do not know. The only one that does not crawl to her sleeping hole until she finds me my gems."

As if that's a choice. As if his men don't kill anyone who doesn't dig the gems from that cursed rock.

My teeth clench and my neck stiffens but I keep my head down.

"Bring the beverage," he says, and that's when I lift my gaze to his, anger flashing through my eyes.

He's on a raised platform with three steps leading up to it. It separates him from the dance floor and the rest of the club, where party-goers writhe to the strange music that sounds like a bass guitar mixed in with a xylophone.

He wants me to go to him? Climb...no...*crawl up* the steps like the peasant he sees me as.

The drinks will spill. He *must* know that. There's no way I can balance the tray *and* myself.

But before I can open my mouth, one female standing at his side leaves her position. The words stick in my throat as I recognize her as the nymph-like alien that had been working in the mines with me.

Her eyes are soft, her throat moving as her gaze darts to the side at the Morang, fear evident in how her hands tremble as they take the tray from my hand. My arm collapses the moment the weight is taken from it and she hurries to stand behind the Morang, her small frame barely visible.

My eyes are on her and not the imposing male sitting before her. That's when she nods slightly and understanding dawns.

She helped me because I tried to help her before.

I can't nod back, not when this asshole is looking right at me, but I hope she knows I am thankful.

"Now go for more," the Morang says.

My gaze slides to his and my teeth grind so hard, I fear they might crack. Whatever he sees on my face only makes him laugh. It is a strange sound that comes off more like a hiss.

He's toying with me.

Turning slowly, I fight the pain in my limbs as I pull myself back in the bar's direction.

His cruelty almost breaks me.

But I swallow any tears welling in my eyes, I ignore the beings whose gazes slide to the human pulling herself across the floor, and I go for the asshole's drinks.

He will tire of this game soon, and then what? He'll send me to the mines? Or will he do something equally terrifying?

For the hundredth time, my gaze slides to the door where streams of partygoers enter, and I halt for a moment, staring at it. I can't go through there. It's too busy. But, if I could run, I would go for it. I would run for freedom. For my life.

"Another set?" A soft voice asks, and I glance up at the bar before me. Three beings who'd come for drinks almost stumble over me and stop themselves just in time. Ignoring their stares and surprised gasps when they're this close is hard.

"Another set." I force a smile at the bartender. He's the same species as the light-blue male I'd been beside down in the mine. And he's been the only face of kindness I've seen in this place, apart from that nymph. Grabbing two drinks, he sets them on a tray and brings them around the bar and down to my level.

I take a moment, gathering my energy before I set up myself to carry the tray back to the Morang boss. Only when I have the tray steady on my palm does the bartender give me a tight, sorrowful kind of smile before going back to his duties.

Releasing a steady breath, I begin my journey back toward the Morang boss.

This trip is harder than the others. My body aches, my chest heaves, and it's hard to breathe.

I am tired, but I dare not stop.

Only, I am forced to when a set of dark boots suddenly blocks my path.

Fuck these Morang and their boss and their stupid mine.

Frowning, I tilt my head upward, ready to pin a glare on the asshole who has blocked my path *on purpose.*

But as my gaze moves up from the boots, going up the dark trou, to the dark tunic and higher, my anger turns to confusion.

Bronze skin peeks out at the neck of the tunic, followed by the face of the most handsome man—alien—*being*—I have ever seen in my life. A firm jaw complemented by high cheekbones…and golden eyes that seem to glow in the light that catches them. Shoulder-length white hair frames his gorgeous face and I'm on the floor, but I know that if I was standing, the top of my head would probably only meet his chest.

My eyes widen and the tray with the drinks falls to the floor as my hand goes slack.

Who is this male?

He's looking at me as if he's seen a ghost, and, at the same time, I watch as those golden eyes of his become filled with what can only be rage.

My gaze falls immediately as the liquid from the drinks soaks into what's left of my blouse.

Only then do I realize that, in my surprise and possibly awe, I'd dumped the contents of the tray right on this god's boots.

4

Qhenno

Gods of Atar…I have found the human.

As soon as I step into the Morang's entertainment cove, any hesitation I might have felt while docking my shuttle and heading into this uncertainty dissipates when I set my eyes on her.

There, right before me, is the human. *On the qeffing floor.*

Crawling, she stops at the bar, and the bartender hands her a tray with beverages. Anger brims in my lifeblood as she struggles to balance them before her body heaves with a heavy breath.

I can tell she's exhausted. That the disgusting Morang have been working her to the bone, and that she's close to breaking down.

Still, she steadies herself and turns.

Something wrings deep inside me.

Her legs. They don't work.

She is here, working in the mines, serving the Morang beverages, *and they haven't even had the decency to give her a mobility aid.*

It comes fast, and it comes strong—rage so intense I don't know its source. And when the human turns and bumps into me, spilling the beverages all across herself, I don't even notice that she's spilled them over me too.

It's only when her soft voice, filled with anxiety and nervousness, filters through the noise and reaches my ears that I realize she's frantically trying to use the torn linen wrapped around her palms to clean my boot.

"I—I'm sorry. I didn't—I wasn't looking where I was going. I'm sorry. I—I—I'll clean your boots right away." The most beautiful eyes look up at me. Arzentus mixed with brown and green, they dart away from my face as she tries hard to clean my boot, frantic to catch the droplets of fluid coating the material.

I'm suddenly kicked out of whatever trance I'm in, and I stoop, taking her trembling hands in mine. She freezes, going still as if waiting for me to…do something crazy like *harm* her.

That fury boiling in my chest spikes again.

Qeffing Morang. I can only imagine the horrors they have put this soft little female through and the thought makes me growl, loud enough for the Morang around us to cease their writhing movements. Loud enough to bring attention to me and the human. But the rage now vibrating through my veins is hard to control. I have never felt such red-hot fury.

"P-Please," the human whispers, her eyes darting to the side, dark brown hair that twirls to her shoulder flashing as her head whips. She's noticed that more and more partygoers have stopped to look our way. "I don't want any trouble. Let me clean your boots. I can get them dry."

She tries to pull her hands from mine, frantic to attend to me, but I can't let her go. My fury mixes with her distress, swirling within me to create a poisoning concoction that makes me want to rip into every Morang in our presence.

I want to speak. To tell her she doesn't have to worry about my stupid boots. That I'm here to get her out of this…*somehow.* But my tongue has rolled into a ball in my throat.

Despite the rage, the danger around us, and that this isn't the time for proper greetings or introductions, I am frozen in a moment of wrath…and awe. I cannot pull my eyes away from her face.

Her hands, soft in my grasp, tremble. Her face, a mirror of growing panic.

I want to reassure her. Tell her I am here now…but…something is possibly actually wrong with my tongue. No words come forth. Only wild, crashing emotions that hit me unprepared.

I expected to be upset when I found her…but not like this.

When a single bead of water runs down the human's cheek, something deep inside me wrings again. It is like all else is forgotten around us. I don't care about the qeffing Morang or the fact that I am surrounded by them.

All I can see is her pain…and an overwhelming urge to take that pain away from her engulfs me.

She winces but doesn't pull away when I lift a finger to wipe the eye waters away. Those enchanting orbs of hers rise hesitantly up to my face, her gaze searching mine as confusion fills her eyes.

"What is this?!" The words echo in what is now a silent room, causing the female before me to jerk in surprise. The annoying music has stopped. The revelers have ceased their writhing. All eyes are on me and the human…and I can only stare at her, my back stiffening with knowledge there is danger all around us.

Again, she tries to pull her hands from mine, her gaze flicking down at the liquid spilled across the floor and the tray that lies toppled within it, and I can almost taste her fear.

She is dirty, she looks like she hasn't eaten in days, and I can see countless cuts and scrapes on her skin. But even with all this, she is so…delicate. Beautiful. Something precious that should be cradled and kept safe.

"Who dares to enter my domain and interfere with one of my slaves?" The Morang boss' voice sounds louder than before and my lips pull back in a snarl, my fangs extending as I turn in the direction of the sound.

I spot him immediately.

There, seated on a platform raised above the floor where the revelers frolic, he sits watching over everything. And as if his elevated position isn't enough for him to see everything happening in his little pleasure domain, the crowd has parted, creating a direct line of sight between him and me.

I see the moment his dark eyes widen in his eye sockets. The scales at the side of his throat shift in color—a display of anxiety or aggression. Most likely the latter.

I know little about the Morang. They keep to themselves, trading their precious jewels, but can be a ruthless enemy if you make them one.

And here I am. In a room surrounded by Morang and one of their leaders.

They are no friends of the Atari, and that's clear from how the air has suddenly grown thick and heavy. The sensitive skin at the back of my neck tightens.

I should not have come here. Bhihan was right. *But I am here now.* And I am not leaving without the female at my side. Her small hand tightens in mine, tension radiating through her, and I force myself to calm, *for her sake.*

There's no telling how I will extract us from this mess. Even in the few moments of the Morang boss spotting us, three Morang guards have taken position at the exit, weapons in hand.

We won't be leaving this place without someone being slaughtered. Or…we won't be leaving this place at all.

I've spent too long at the helm of the Zarzenius, taking us through countless missions and unknown battlefields to not see what's coming.

This Morang…has taken interest in the human. He has her crawling to serve him while he has many other more capable slaves who could do a more efficient job. For some reason, he has chosen *her* to do it.

My ear twitches and I note the movement of three more guards off in the crowd to my right.

We're surrounded, even without counting the civilian Morang who are here for entertainment. The chances of me getting the human and myself out of here alive are close to nil. If I was alone…I could do this…But I have found her. And I cannot afford for her to be harmed.

That only leaves one other option…

I must surrender. For now.

"An *Atari*?" the Morang boss says. He stands, and the females catering to him shuffle out of his path as he walks down to floor level. "What is an Atari doing here? In my midst?"

His gaze flicks around the room as if he's checking whether I am alone.

I couldn't enter the venue without my weapons being stripped. Only my communicator remains hidden in a pocket of my trou.

I am as harmless as an Atari warrior can be.

"To what do we Morang owe this…*pleasure*?" The Morang boss says the word as if it is bitter on his forked tongue.

My nostrils flare with hardly controlled fury as I track his gait.

His movements are smooth. They don't betray the fact he can dart forward at any minute and slice through my throat if he wishes.

Adjusting myself so I can roll out of the way and take the female with me should he attack, I continue to watch him move.

But he doesn't strike. He walks, the room so silent his every step can be heard, until he is standing two arm lengths away from me. Far enough to react if I attack, but close enough to not appear cowardly.

"You have taken something of mine," I say to him.

Whispers fill the room and the Morang boss' eyes narrow almost imperceptibly.

"*Taken*?" he repeats. "We Morang never *take*," he says. "We *conquer*." His lips split into something that should be a smile. Instead, it comes off as more of a snarl and there are grunts of approval in the otherwise silent crowd. "Whatever you see here, Atari, I own."

"*Not this female.*" The words leave my mouth before I can consider them and I tell myself it is merely a reaction to seeing a female treated so horribly. I tell myself that I would do this for any other female I rescue and that my rage has nothing to do with the small squeezes the human is delivering to my hand, or the way I can hear her every nervous breath, or feel the shivers going through her. Her skin is so thin, I can feel her pulse hammering through her hand that's squeezing mine.

I meet the Morang's gaze. "She belongs to *me—us*. She is a female of Atar, protected by the Atari."

The room seems to chill with my words and I don't think any of the

Morang breathe until their leader lets out a hiss, those patches of skin under his neck pulsing, the color getting increasingly red.

"This is *my* city," he growls. "Have you forgotten you have stepped onto my lands?"

He takes another step forward and halts, his gaze flicking over me, probably looking for hidden weapons.

I keep my gaze on him, pretending I don't notice the increasing number of guards lining the edges of the room.

"I am only here to retrieve the female I came for…not to start a war."

The Morang boss tilts his head slightly, and I shift so he can't stare at the female at my back. But he knows she is there. He knows exactly which female I am referring to.

"*That* broken thing?"

"*Broken*?" My fist tightens, and it is only the insistent fear coming from the human at my back that stops me from releasing her to define the word broken for him.

His arms. Both legs. I will make him crawl like he has made her do before I break his skull, too.

Unaware of the thoughts going through my mind, he glances at the revelers behind him with an air of confidence. Each one of them is like a soldier at his back.

I shouldn't have come here. I should have let Bhihan come so his cold heart could freeze them over. But that insistent pull that guided me here is still there, even stronger now. I have found the female, and if I didn't come for her, I am sure we would have lost her forever.

When the Morang boss laughs, his hiss carries across the room. "Friends, it seems the rumors of Atar's fertility problem are true. They will risk their lives for just anything so they can mate with it."

Qef breaking his skull. I will *shatter* it.

My fist tightens some more. That's when a soft whisper behind me reaches my ears.

"What are you doing? They will *kill* you," the human whispers.

Her voice is like a velvety shadow that whispers over my ears.

She's probably right. But something else is pulling me forward.

Like a rope I have no control over. It's an urge as strong as my will to breathe.

I need to protect her.

I will.

I must.

The Morang boss sobers and his cold gaze settles on me once more. "An Atari dares to come into my midst and challenge me..." he states. "For something I own."

My eyebrow twitches. I haven't challenged him. *Yet.* And I will. He will pay for what he has done to her.

"I will compensate you for her release," I say. "How much do you want?"

His gaze twinkles for only a second. "You have Karmachi gems?"

My jaw clenches. "I have Arzentus. I have Galactic credits. You only trade Karmachi gems among you Morang. You do not trade it outside your realm."

"Ah," he says, "but we do. You Atari only pretend to not like the things we trade them for."

My brows furrow some more.

Slaves and other items the Galactic Union has outlawed, no doubt.

The Morang leader studies me for just a moment before turning as if to walk away from us. With one flick of his arm, three guards appear from the shadows. The human's grasp is ripped from mine as one of them grabs her from behind. Her screech makes my life organ tighten as I spin, my fist moving forward to land in the nose of the Morang who has his claws on her, but the remaining two guards grab hold of my arms.

I stare at the female. I see her fear. And once again, I calculate the chance of her being harmed if I decide to fight. It is too high, and I know getting her out of this will take much more than bartering.

"A thousand credits," I say, knowing the Morang boss is still close enough to hear. There's a gasp in the crowd and I sense the moment when he turns to look back at me.

"Even if you say five thousand, this female is much too valuable."

Five thousand? That could buy him an unlimited number of slaves. Why turn down such an offer?

"This female has the vision," he says, his voice coming closer. "She finds the gems when others can't. Not one cycle has passed where she hasn't found me a gem." He moves closer, close enough for me to feel his presence behind me. "After this revolution, I will send her even deeper into the mines, where the rock is hard and the slaves fail. The gems there are big but sit deep. She will work hard to find them. After all, she cannot run. She can only sit and give me what I want."

A sick feeling develops in my chest and I growl loud enough to send a chill in the air. Maybe because of his words. Maybe because of the water that's escaped from the female's eyes once more.

"Throw him out and send her to level four," he continues. "He is wasting my time."

Before his guards can move, I throw my arm back, twisting it enough to get a hold of one of them. He is surprised, not expecting the move, and I take that opportunity to slam my head into his. Pain rockets into my skull, but the effect is worse for him because he didn't expect it. He releases me and staggers back, giving me enough time to twist and plant my knee into his colleague's belly. He doubles over.

There's a scream. The human. Her wide eyes on me. One arm outstretched as she screams again. "No!"

That's when I feel the cool metal pricking into the skin at the back of my neck. My lifeblood seeps from the wound and runs down my back, forcing me to stop moving.

"Atari," the Morang boss says. "The moment you left on this foolish mission, success was futile. I give you this chance to leave and I will consider not killing you. Take this as your final warning."

I can only stare at the female before me. Confusion and sadness flood her gaze, as I watch the little hope that had sprung within it die.

"No," I state.

The whole room falls into another level of silence and the female snaps her gaze to mine.

"What?" It is her that speaks, breaking the silence, her voice an incredulous lilting thing that almost makes me smile.

"Let me take her place. *I* will find you the gems. Enough to line your coffers for ten orbits. Then you will let us go."

The silence is almost deafening, but I know, even before he opens his mouth, that he will accept my request.

No one has ever escaped the Morang mines. Heavily guarded and with only one known exit, I am offering myself up to him on a platter. We both know he can accept my offer and still refuse to let us go. A willing, hardworking slave mining precious gems? It's almost too good to be true.

And he says exactly what I expect him to.

"Take them to the mines."

5

Trudy

It all feels like it's happening so quickly. *Too* quickly.

Where did this dude come from? Who is he? Why does it seem like he's…*bartering* for me? And if he is…*why*?

He just requested to be sent to the mines. *Is he fucking insane?*

As the Morang that grabbed me suddenly releases me, gravity kicks in and I fall. I let out a yelp, stretching my hands out to help stop my inevitable crash into the floor, only, I never meet the ground.

Strong arms surround me, pulling me into a hard chest.

The stranger caught me before I could hit the floor, the weight of my fall not even causing a grunt or strain.

Too stunned to speak, I don't even get to mutter thanks before we are moving, sandwiched between two Morang as we are hustled out the door.

We're going back to the mines. The exact place I've been trying to escape.

My heart thunders in my chest, fear leeching into my bones, the thought of going back into that dark hole making me shudder.

Maybe the stranger thinks I am cold, because he holds me even closer, pressing me into him.

Why didn't he fight to escape? Unlike me, he had a choice to get his ass out of there, and he didn't take it. But even *I* could see that he's a lot stronger than he presented himself. A guy with muscles like his could do a lot of damage.

I'm as confused as I was at the start, when he lifted a finger to wipe my tears away.

He adjusts me in his grasp, unintentionally pulling me closer, and a soft, fresh scent whispers across my nose. I take a deep inhale without meaning to. He smells clean and fresh, like a cool tall glass of water, and I'm immediately reminded that I am filthy.

But if I stink, he doesn't give any sign it bothers him.

I look up at him, my gaze traveling over his features, and I'm once again struck speechless. He's...*gorgeous*—with a face that makes little shivers of excitement go through my body. He has the type of face I used to see on ads that played on those huge holoboards lining the ledges leading to the Upper Levels. One of those same ledges I'd slipped and fallen off, causing my life to be taken away from me before it even fully began.

I still remember staring at those boards and imagining myself as one of the beautiful, wealthy females advertised there. Wearing fine clothes and being happy.

That's what he looks like...Like he belongs with people who live like that.

So what the hell is someone like him doing in a place like this?

His gaze flicks down to me so suddenly, my breath stops in my nose. Those rich, golden eyes move over my face, warming, before he turns his gaze back to where we are heading, and I'm pulled back to reality.

This isn't a time to be drooling over some stranger. I'm being sent back into that hole, and worse, *somehow*, I've gotten some innocent dude into this mess, too.

I'm pretty sure he doesn't know what he's signed up for. But even more, the *why* of it all comes right back to the forefront of my mind.

Where did he come from? Who is he? And *why* is he doing this?

There's a clang before the sound of grinding metal meets our ears.

Turning my gaze before us, I see the Morang at the front opening the gate that leads down to the mines. It is only my second time seeing it. The first was just three days ago when the Morang had taken me from the mine shaft.

When I'd first arrived at the mines, I'd been unconscious, and I wonder now if that had been a twist of luck. Because walking down into the dark tunnel that continues to descend lower and lower into the earth is terrifying, even though I know what will greet us at the end.

The Morang at the front turns on a mechanical light that he uses to illuminate the way ahead, and soon there is crunching underfoot as the path changes from smooth to crushed rock.

I glance up at the stranger holding me again and find that he's still staring ahead. His body feels rigid, as if he's tense, and…of course, he is. Maybe he mistook me for someone else? It's going to be a really uncomfortable conversation if that's the case.

"Maria, do not fear, I have come to save you!"

"Maria? My name's not Maria! Wrong chick. Sorry 'bout that."

"Oh no! Have I offered to do all this labor in the hopes of saving the wrong female?!"

"What can I say, bad luck, am I right? Heh."

I almost groan at the thought of it and the urge to hit my forehead against the wall is strong. This is bad. This is very bad.

I know the exact moment we reach the mouth of the mine shaft. The sound of picks digging into the rock, catching, then being pulled out over and over again echoes straight up the column.

I swallow down a lump in my throat. Despite the humiliation I'd received in that club, it was better than this. There's desolation in this mine. A sense that time has stopped, yet, you are here for eternity. I can't believe I'm back here again.

The stranger holding me stiffens as soon as we step on the winding platform that leads down into the pit and I look up at him again.

With a face like his, I can't imagine he's ever had to do work like this before. It makes me wonder even more why he'd offered to come down to the mines. He obviously knows more about our captors than I did at the start. He must know that this is a place where slaves come to die. So why put himself in this position?

His eyes are like warm honey and they move along the walls, over the slaves that we pass, and over the edge of the barrier into the abyss.

Maybe he's looking for something...or *someone*...and a twinge of disappointment flickers through my being.

My lips thin as I press them together while I reason to myself.

It makes sense.

I don't know him. For all I know, he really *is* looking for some alien chick named Maria. The more he scans, his gaze taking every little detail in, the more that thought solidifies.

Possibly, I was just a means to get down into this mine, for whatever reason. His display in front of the Morang boss almost made me believe that by some stroke of luck, he's really come for me. But...no one is coming for me. No one from New Earth and none of my family. Because I have no one left. My mother died a long time ago. I am alone in this.

Down, down, down we go. The platform winding down into the darkness beyond. The familiar stench of sweat and toil fills the air, and I find myself turning slightly so I can inhale more of this stranger's fresh scent.

Eventually, his clean soapy smell will go too, only to be replaced by the same scent permeating this place.

When I recognize the old alcove I used to stay in, I almost open my mouth to stop the Morang. But they already filled the alcove with two resting slaves. My spot has been taken. They weren't kidding when they said they were going to send us even lower into the mine.

Shit.

I swallow hard as we go even deeper. It's colder the lower we go, and I can't seem to escape the increasing tension in my gut.

If I thought escape was bleak before...I was wrong. Now, there is really no chance.

The Morang halts before us and grunts, gesturing to one of the few alcoves this deep into the mine shaft. It's just big enough to hold two people and I glance up at the bronze god holding me again, my eyes widening slightly when I see his lips curl in disgust.

Wait till he sees where we use the toilet.

There's another clang that jerks my attention away from him and I look back at the Morang to see he's thrown two picks into the alcove.

"Next shift starts in six yoras…*Atari*."

Right. Atari. They'd said that in the club as well. The bronze god is Atari…but that name does nothing to help me understand who he is. I have never heard of the Atari. On the Lower Levels, up-to-date news of what's going on outside New Earth is scarce.

"Ensure you are at your station." The Morang growls before gesturing to two open spots in between two slaves. It's not too far from the alcove and I release a breath of relief. At least I won't have to drag myself very far across the floor to reach my work area.

"*What do you expect her to sleep on?*" the Atari growls, his fangs flashing. He seems to be barely controlling his anger and I realize it's the reason his muscles have been so tense. "The cold, hard rock?"

The Morang studies him for a second, those cold unfeeling eyes giving nothing away. He tilts his head forward, coming dangerously close to us. So close, I can feel the brush of his scales against my arm and I cower into the Atari holding me.

I expect the Atari to step back at this outward display of aggression, but his muscles only tighten and he doesn't budge.

"You belong to the Morang now, *foolish* Atari," the Morang says. "Guard your tongue."

The Atari growls again, his hands tightening almost painfully against my skin as his brows dive so severely they look like they will cut into his forehead.

I half-expect him to headbutt the Morang like he'd done before and my heart thumps a little harder at that thought. We are on the rickety platform. If a fight breaks out now, someone will fall over. And it will probably be us. The Morang behind us might be silent, but I feel his presence like a cold, dark cloud.

They outnumber us.

Demonstrating his dominance, the Morang at the front snarls, displaying sharp teeth before he brushes past us, walking on the inside. It causes the Atari to shift toward the edge of the platform and my eyes bulge as I stare down into the abyss. It's only for a second and the Atari soon rights my position, his piercing gaze on the back of the Morang as they make their way back up the platform.

If his eyes could shoot daggers, they'd both be dead.

As we are left in the presence of only the few other slaves this low in the shaft, I stare at the Atari, waiting for his next move. So do the slaves closest to us as well. Covert glances shoot our way. Some intrigued, some confused.

I fully expect him to drop me now that he doesn't have to put on a show.

I'm mistaken.

A surprised sound leaves my lips when he suddenly crouches and enters the alcove, still cradling me in his arms.

He utters something akin to a curse. It is like a whisper on his lips as he sets me down. I let out a slow breath, bracing on my elbows as I shuffle backward, putting as much distance as I can between us to give him some space. The floor is smooth from years of slaves sleeping in the same spot, but it is uneven and the walls are jagged. It is just like the last alcove I had shared with some other slaves. It isn't great for sleeping, but it's better than staying on the platform. One reckless doze and I'd fall down the shaft.

As I pause my shuffling, I look up at the Atari. The darkness and the entrance of the alcove frame him; yet, I can see the warm honey of those eyes as he stares at me.

"I—" I begin, but words fail me. I don't know what to say to this male. And he is silent. Only that heated gaze regards me, slowly morphing from one filled with rage into something else as he continues to stare at me. His gaze grows warm…surprise, no, *shock* clearly communicated in those eyes as he stares at me.

"Th-thank you for carrying me down here." I give him a hesitant smile. "It would have been difficult for me otherwise, as you can probably tell…"

My words trail off as I stare back at him.

Fuck, his gaze is intense.

Gone is all the rage and fury.

He's looking at me as if I am someone he never thought he'd see again. But that's…that's impossible. I've never met him before. If I did, I'd definitely remember.

My cheeks warm for some reason, and a tingly feeling develops in my belly.

I feel like I'm under the spotlight and I fist and unfist my hands, gripping my blouse in the spots where it hasn't been torn.

His gaze shifts to that movement and I stop immediately, my fingers going still. Without saying a word, the Atari moves the rest of the way into the alcove. He fills it completely. No way we're going to share this space without someone being crushed against the rock wall.

"We will probably have to take shifts working," I whisper, my gaze slipping over his broad shoulders. Was he this huge from the start? "I will stay outside and search for those gems while you rest…so you can have the space and be comfortable." I pause. "Well, as comfortable as you can be in this place."

He freezes, his brows furrowing.

He still hasn't said anything.

Is he upset with me or something?

Probably… After all, he's down here because, for some reason I still can't ascertain, he tried to help me.

Shuffling over toward the jagged wall that frames the space, I shift my gaze to the darkness as I try to give him room, but there's not much to give. I hardly make enough space between us, and the Atari says nothing.

"I hope you don't mind sharing with me." I pull my bottom lip into my mouth, wondering just what to say to this male. I have no idea what he's thinking. "You don't have to worry about me getting in your way."

He makes a soft sound, one so low I almost don't catch it, and when my gaze flicks to him, I swear the bronze skin across his cheeks has gotten darker. Or it might just be my eyes. My eyesight is average at best.

There's a shuffling sound as he moves farther into the alcove, probably to rest before our shift starts, but when he simply moves to kneel by me…

I frown as I watch him, wondering if the dim lights of the torches outside are playing tricks on me. But as the hem of his tunic lifts, my lips fall open and my eyes bug out.

"What are you—"

Perfect abs, the shadows playing under the ridges of those muscles, greet my eyes. As he pulls his head out of the tunic and shakes his hair, those startling eyes fall on me once more and something twinges deep inside my belly again. Little butterflies feel like they tickle my gut.

Damn. How long has it really been since I've been stuck in this mine shaft? I shouldn't be reacting to him like this, pretty face or not.

The tunic shakes in his hand as the Atari thrusts it in my direction and my eyes bug out even more.

"Wha— You're giving me your clothes?" I glance at him, at the arm outstretched with the tunic, then back. It's cold in this cavern and any sane person would hoard any clothing they can get. But here he is handing me the only piece of cloth on his back. "I...I can't take that."

He thrusts it toward me again, his throat moving as if he wants to say something. All that happens is him clearing his throat, his eyes burning into mine as the color across his cheeks darkens.

His gaze may be warmer, but his jaw is ticking as if he is still fucking pissed. So, I swallow hard and take the tunic from his hand in case rejecting his offer is what's making him tick like a time bomb.

Oh Lord...just *who* is this dude?

It's soft, the tunic. Softer than it looks, and that same soapy scent is embedded in it. I almost press it to my nose and inhale. Only the strangeness of the situation stops me from doing anything more than stare back at him like a wide-eyed bug.

"Thanks?" I whisper.

He barely jerks his chin to accept my gratitude before his gaze slowly slips down my frame, traveling over my belly and down to my legs.

My skin tingles, and there is an immediate urge to hide. Instead, I freeze. I wait for the disgust to reflect on his face, like how his lips curled earlier when interacting with the Morang.

But...none of that happens...

I see a thousand emotions pass through those golden eyes...and not one of them is disgust.

He creeps closer, almost painfully slowly as if I am a mouse and he's scared if he moves too fast I'll scamper away. Eyes meeting mine, he reaches for my hands and I'm caught in a trance as he takes them into his own.

Warm. His fingers are so warm, they make mine feel like ice sticks.

He pries the tunic from my fingers and sets it down in my lap before turning my palms upward.

His jaw ticks again, and maybe it pulls me from my trance, because I finally jerk back to reality and realize just how close he's come.

I try to pull my hands away, just out of the sheer shock of him holding them, but he doesn't let go. My brain feels like it's stuttering and unable to focus. His hold on me is gentle. So much so that when I try to pull my hands away, his come along with me.

When I look up at him, he's watching me as if he's waiting for my permission. If that's the case, why doesn't he say something? I can't read his mind…or maybe I can, because when I give him a hesitant nod, relaxing my hand in his, his throat moves as he swallows hard and does the strangest thing.

I don't know what I expected him to do. I guess I thought he was just looking at the blackened and torn strips of my blouse that I'd wrapped across my palm. They're the only thing to protect it from the sharp shards of rock I have to work with.

Maybe he likes the idea and plans to make some for himself?

But it's not the cloth he's interested in.

Slowly, and with gentle care, he sets one of my hands in my lap as he strips the cloth from the other to reveal my palm. Now I should really pull my hand away. It's filled with callouses and cuts. It's not the prettiest sight, but I'd long stopped caring about the state of my palms when my need for survival took the forefront of my mind.

His fingers brush over the callouses, making my palms tingle.

"It's not as bad as it looks." For some reason, I'm whispering, but I can't find it in myself to speak any louder with him so close. "If you do what I did with the cloth, it will protect your hands a little." I jerk my chin to the tunic in my lap. "You can have it back if you want."

The only thing I get from him is a grunt, one that sounds filled with displeasure before his gaze meets mine again.

He stares at me with a look that's filled with sorrow and rage. The sort of look you'd give someone you care about deeply when you find out they've been harmed by another.

This time, when I try to pull my hands away, he lets me.

"I…" I begin.

I don't know what else to say. This whole situation is too confusing and the fact he won't speak to me isn't helping either. It makes me feel…like this is all my fault even though I know it isn't.

"I should go start working," I say, dipping my head even though I can still feel his gaze on me. "The faster I find the gems, the better. And you can stay here and take your rest before the shift starts. I'm sure they'll check on us as soon as it's time."

Reaching down, I grab one of my legs so I can twist myself and crawl out of the alcove, but a warm hand closes over my wrist, and another on my shoulder.

With gentle insistence, the Atari pushes me backward, fury in his gaze as he stares at me.

He holds me there, our gazes locked, until he seems satisfied that I won't move.

And then he…leaves.

He scrambles from the alcove without a word, grabs the picks, and he's gone.

6

Qhenno

By the gods…what is wrong with me?

Out in the stale air of this cavern, I try not to look back into the alcove as I stand between two slaves already working. The sounds of the slaves working, picks clanging into rock, distant echoes of the Morang guards shouting, and random coughs all fade into the background as my life organ thunders in my chest.

That soft skin at the back of my neck heats and pulses. My body feels like it's becoming ill. I have to fight from trembling as I set the pick into the rock wall before me.

Taking a deep breath, I try to clear my head.

I'd thought it was the Morang and their loathsomeness that had ticked me off. That seeing the human in such a position, a precious female no less, was what had woken up something deep inside me.

But no, this is something much more.

Something is happening that I…I can't explain.

Maybe I *am* becoming ill. If the Morang have exposed me to some pathogen…

But even as the thought appears, I know it is wrong. There is no pathogen. If that were the case, the slaves around me would succumb to the same thing. There are so many species stuck in this mine—more than I could count on the way down into the pit. Some females. Mostly males.

Slamming the pick into the rock one more time, some shards break off and fall at my feet.

Sharp, this rock. It doesn't crumble but falls in thin strips that will slice into you if you're not careful. Slice into *her*.

She'd been smart to wrap her soft hands in strips of her garment. Even then, she has suffered from this horrible work.

There are dark circles under her beautiful eyes, and her skin is so pale that every bruise inflicted upon it stands out like a marker of the pain she's been through.

Seeing her wounds…hearing her speak, planning on how to make my time here with her as smooth as possible…I could hardly take it.

Like a coward, I had to move away from her for her safety, because only one thing was on my mind.

Protect this female. Take her pain.

And the only way I could think of doing that was to pull her into my arms and soothe her.

But the moment I'd set her down, she'd pulled herself away from me.

I'm a stranger to her. She doesn't want to be near me…and she's right not to trust someone who's come into her life from nowhere.

Qef.

I slam the pick into the rock again, burying it deep, the glances of the other slaves around me hardly registering in my mind. They look at me, their gazes flicking down my form, probably wondering how I ended up down in this pit.

I almost chuckle.

If Bhihan finds out about this, he won't let me live it down. But this is only a minor setback. I'm getting out of this. One opening is all I need. I have the sole reason for this mission right here with me now— the human—and that's all that matters.

I won't let her out of my sight.

My gaze slides to the alcove and I swear I see her jerk her head back inside, as if she'd crept to the entrance to look at me.

The warmth at the back of my neck pulses and I have to roll my shoulders to alleviate some of the tension.

If she thinks she's going to take up one of these picks again, she's mistaken. I will find us both gems, and I'm only doing it to buy us time. I will strap her to my back and wrap her arms around me, if only to prevent them from doing this work anymore.

The thought makes warmth go directly to my shaft and I freeze, the feeling both surprising and intense. She's so small. So soft. I can just imagine what it would feel like to have her pressed against my back.

My fangs extend enough to nick my lips and I slam the pick into the stone, flicking my tongue out to wipe the faint taste of lifeblood away.

If I have it my way, she won't get anywhere near these picks or this rock. Qef. I want her out of this hole…

But she doesn't know that. And why? Because I'm a qeffing idiot.

I couldn't even speak to her. Like a kit, I froze the moment we were alone. When my focus was solely on her and she overwhelmed my senses.

The way tendrils of her hair are soft, but tangled, my fingers itching to thread through them and make them blow in the wind again. The way the cold reddens her soft, pale face. The way she pulls her plump lower lip into her mouth when she's thinking. The way her eyes seem filled with water that refuses to fall…and how she looked at me. So many questions in her gaze. Questions I should have answered…but couldn't.

Swallowing hard, I feel the lump in my throat as if she is right before me again. The skin at the back of my neck thickens and heats, thought of her making my pulse quicken.

Something *is* wrong with me. Maybe there is a pathogen after all. One that affects only Atari?

That skin at the back of our necks only gets irritated when we are in immediate danger, or when…

No…

It couldn't be…

The gasp and shuffle of one of the slaves closest to me is the only thing that makes me realize I dropped the pick. It skitters down the platform and falls off the side into the abyss. I watch it go, one thought now at the forefront of my mind that supersedes everything else.

Far off in the distance, in the back of my mind somewhere behind the clangs of picks digging into rock, I hear the Morang shout. But as I stare into the abyss, my breath thundering in my lungs so hard that my chest heaves, I can only see one thing in my mind's eye.

The female.

Thought of her makes the skin at the back of my neck pulse once more, heat flooding through me.

My...mate?

I blink, remaining frozen as I stare into the darkness.

The pulsing at the back of my neck. The urge to protect this female I've only just met with *my life*. Could it be?

Falling to my knees, the platform rocks and the slaves behind me let out sounds of fear and surprise.

"He's going to jump over," one of them says.

"We should stop him...sh-shouldn't we?"

"The Morang won't care. What if we interfere and get punished for the fact?"

Their concerned whispers reach my ears but are of no consequence.

My mate...

Have I...have I found the one thing I have been craving since...forever?

My life organ beats so hard, I can't hear anything over the pulse in my ears.

Even before I saw her, the signs were there. The fates knew. They led me here.

And even knowing that...it is hard to believe. For though I have wanted a mate more than anything...*craved* it...some part of me believed it would never happen.

My homeworld, Atar, is blessed with male kin. Females are scarce.

Countless male Atari like me can only dream of finding a mate. If I could only be so lucky...

As I stare into the abyss, thoughts of the impossible finally coming within my grasp, something twinkles enough to reach my gaze. It is only slight, the light, and at first, I think it is a tool that fell over catching some of the dim light in this place.

But no…

I stare at the small twinkle of light, the most recent revelation still causing my legs to go weak.

Qef. It was good I didn't realize this while I'd been carrying the female down into this hole. I might have collapsed with her in my arms out of pure joy.

The female…

I groan.

I don't even know her name, but this all explains why I couldn't speak. My body knew before my mind could catch on.

This entire time, I'd been searching for what's wholly and completely mine. A treasure for me to keep close. To love. To cherish.

And I have finally found her.

But something wrings in my chest.

I have found her…*but I have failed her*.

She's been stuck in this place, this desolate cold hole for only the fates know how long. A male is supposed to keep his female safe. Well fed. Surrounded by all the comforts her mind dreams of.

Will she even accept me now?

Releasing a breath, I try to steady myself.

I was the one piloting the Zarzenius when we went to collect the Earthkin. If I had been faster…if I had known…I could have prevented her all this pain. We would be happy on Atar, nestled in my quarters, while I made sure every inch of her buzzed and tingled with warmth.

We are far from that place.

I have indeed failed her before I had the chance to show her the care she deserves. Yes…there's a good chance she will reject me now. But even if she doesn't accept me…if she rejects the mate bond, I will still be by her side. I will take her from this mess. I will make sure she is happy and safe…regardless if I get to share in that happiness or not.

Rising, I'm about to turn away from the abyss when that twinkle deep in the dark pit catches my gaze again.

I frown, leaning closer to the edge, almost putting my whole upper body over so I can see. I hear the slaves behind me gasp. One grabs on to my leg, his whisper insistent as he pleads for me not to go over.

"*What are you doing*?" he hisses and I turn to see a Cambrian male, eyes wide as he stares at me. He is light blue, a little smaller than I am, and furless. "*If you go over, you will meet certain death.*"

My lips twist a little into a smile and the Cambrian's face distorts into one of unsurety—as if he's wondering if I have gone insane.

I grin at him, a laugh bubbling from my chest as I pull myself away from the edge. Everyone around us freezes, their gazes flicking to me. They assume the same as the Cambrian.

That I have gone mad.

And, granted, I might be somewhat out of my mind.

Eyes focusing on the alcove, I catch the beautiful gaze of my mate before she ducks back inside.

My grin widens.

For I have found my mate…and a way out of this hellhole.

7

Trudy

Dear universe, what in the hell is happening?

I watched the hot god creep to the edge of the platform as if he was about to throw himself off. Only the grip of that familiar light-blue male stopped him from falling over.

And then he laughed…laughed like he's insane. *No one laughs in this grave.*

Oh god…I should have realized before.

Him storming into the club, *rescuing* me even though he doesn't know me, *offering* to work in the mine…it's all been one gigantic neon sign that he's not right in the head.

When he turns from the abyss, he locks eyes with me and I duck back into the alcove. I've never pulled my legs so fast over the uneven ground as I am doing now, and I sense his presence at the alcove's entrance as soon as I reach the far end of our small sleeping space.

Setting myself back into the darkness, I reach down and lift my legs to the side, just so they aren't in the way, and I watch him, my gaze wary. I have no clue what he's going to do now.

What I don't expect is for him to climb into the alcove, only far enough that his huge frame is just barely inside as he stops at my feet.

Eyes wide, I watch him for his next move.

But he's only gazing at me, that heat I thought I'd spotted before growing in those golden pits.

His gaze slides down my frame and I shiver.

Smoldering, those eyes. As if, should I hold his gaze too long, I will burn up in their intensity.

Swallowing hard, my breaths become shorter as we stare at each other.

It doesn't take long for me to realize just *how* he is looking at me…

As if he wants to strip my clothes off and lick me from head to toe.

The thought is alarming, and my eyes widen as I fight the strange feeling beginning in my gut. Closing my fists in my lap, I stiffen my shoulders, bitter memories rushing back and chasing away the warmth that was growing in my belly.

I've seen that look before. Too many times before. And it makes something inside me harden immediately.

Where I come from…where a good wage is scarce in a world that's tried to hide the fact you exist…when you're not part of the elites and have to do whatever you can to survive…that look has only meant one thing.

Is that why he tried to save me? It all seems like too much just to get something so easily garnered elsewhere…

Men that look like him only come to Lower Earth for one thing. To satisfy some sick fantasy or to get a cheap time in bed from the poor commoners that live there.

I lived through that. For years, I saw what it did to my mother. Saw how it slowly killed her soul…and I vowed to not let it happen to me.

I frown at the alien before me, my jaw tightening when that look in his eyes only seems to intensify.

"Is it my turn now?" I ask.

He doesn't answer, and when his gaze falls to my lips, I tighten them into a thin line.

"Do you want to use the alcove?" I ask. But again, he says nothing. He stares at me, his throat moving, but he doesn't speak.

Fuck.

My signals are all messed up. Despite hating what that look in his eyes possibly means, my belly is fluttering like I'm a teen. I should take a hint and stop trying to converse with this alien. He's not going to answer me, and I'm not giving him what he wants.

Leaning forward, I grab one of my legs and pull it towards me. I better get out there and start digging. Time is of the essence.

Find those green gems they want. Ensure my safety until I can find a way out of here.

I repeat the mantra I've whispered to myself a thousand times as I lean forward to pull my other leg toward me. But as my hands close around my calf, the Atari suddenly moves, one of his hands closing around mine.

I freeze, only one emotion flying to the forefront.

Anger.

"What is your problem?"

Of course, he doesn't answer.

"I have no clue who you are. No clue where you came from. No clue what the hell you're doing here."

Still, no response, but his fingers tighten slightly on my wrist.

I want to give him the benefit of the doubt. That my body isn't what he wants. It would be a stupid thing for him to get himself thrown into this mine, dooming himself, just for that.

But then again…he's a bit insane, isn't he…?

I release a breath. "Look, I get it, alright. You mistook me for someone else. I'm sorry…but that's not my fault. I really wish I was the female you came here looking for." My shoulders sink as those words hit me with full force.

Who wouldn't want a guy like him storming in and rescuing them? If I had someone like him coming to save me, things wouldn't seem so hopeless.

But I don't…and that's just the reality of it all.

When I try to pull my hand away one more time and he doesn't release me, I glare at him. *"What do you want from me?!"*

He seems to quail a little, his throat working, and maybe it's the intensity of this whole ordeal, too many pent up emotions looking for a way out...because my eyes water, tears springing into them even as I stiffen my shoulders and tighten my jaw.

I'm not going to cry.

What the *fuck* is wrong with me?

Even when I woke up in this cold dark mine, I hadn't cried. Why now?

Just when a tear I can't hold back slips down my cheek, I see him...*shatter.*

His shoulders slump, a sound leaving his throat as fear flashes through his eyes. He crouches lower, low enough for him to bend and wipe my tear away with his free hand.

His touch is so gentle, I'm tempted to tilt my head into his palm, but I fight those wayward emotions and stiffen even more.

What sort of game is this?

"My beautiful *ari*," he finally says, and my eyes widen at the sound of his voice. "I apologize."

His voice... It is nothing like the voice he used with the Morang—clipped and full of big, pissed-off alien.

This voice is low, deep, almost comforting if I wasn't still so wary.

"I have failed you much already..." he says.

I blink at him. "Wh-what?" Failed me? What's he talking about?

Fighting to reconcile the person I'm creating him to be with the male before me is hard.

My brows furrow as my anger dissipates, and I search his gaze. He's so gentle when he cups my cheek that I swallow hard, my mouth opening slightly as I look up at him.

He releases a slow breath, his fingers lingering on my cheek. "I think it is time I tell you everything."

A lump forms in my throat immediately, the skin along my spine tingling. His voice holds sorrow and some trepidation, as if whatever he is about to tell me is news I *don't* want to hear. Or, maybe, news I *need* to hear.

I shift a little as he enters the alcove, crawling in to sit beside me.

I glance at him before adjusting myself and wrapping my arms around my middle.

The Atari releases a slow breath, rubbing the back of his neck as if it hurts, before glancing at me again.

"I didn't mistake you for someone else," he begins.

That only leaves one other possibility...the one I've been trying to deny. The one that makes my stomach shrink and fold in on itself. That he's looking at me so intently because he wants something I refuse to give.

"I came here hoping I would find you before the Morang sent you back to the mine," he continues. "I have been searching for you for so long."

What? My world glitches like one of those old music players back when Earth was just called "Earth".

My lids flicker as I blink several times. "I...don't understand."

"You left your world on what you thought was a cruise. A luxury cruise organized by your world leaders." He runs a hand over his face, his gaze falling to my folded arms.

I can only stare at him. How did he know that?

"When the Khuru attacked your ship, they slaughtered everyone on board. Only four of you survived the attack. We have been searching for you since."

My heart stutters and then beats again. I continue blinking at him, hoping he'll say more. Because I didn't just hear him say what he just said...right?

"I am sorry I have taken so long to find you, my *ari*. I have failed in that regard." He meets my gaze while he says this and I feel warmth flood through me. Warmth that makes me confused as a sense of hope I've tried not to lean on surfaces once more.

Someone was out there looking for us? *Searching* for us?

"You have been through much..." he continues. "More than any female should ever encounter. I want you to know that, on Atari honor, we have given your fellow Earthkin a proper burial."

That horrible morning...when those strange aliens charged into the ship and began slaughtering everyone...

Just as in my nightmares, the screams return to my consciousness. The chaos.

I still don't know why I survived.

But I am happy to know I am not the only one that did.

Relief causes those tears that had welled in my eyes to grow bigger and the male freezes, pain entering his gaze as he stares at me.

Just looking at him, seeing the care plastered on his face, such a strong emotion that he doesn't seem to care to hide, opens the floodgates and tears run down my cheeks.

"Sorry," I mutter, wiping them away. "I don't know what's wrong with me."

But I know exactly what is wrong with me.

All this time, I've forced myself to push through, to not think of the terrible slaughter that happened on that ship, to not *remember*. But here he is, telling me that others survived. That I wasn't the only one spared from that horrible death, and, what's more, that *he* has been searching for me this whole time.

I brush a hand across my cheek, desperate to wipe my tears away, but they don't stop. The more I wipe, the more they come.

"Fuck," I mutter, desperately trying to compose myself and sniffling as I do.

I'm usually stronger than this. I don't know what about this male is causing my barriers to drop so quickly.

I want to ask him questions. I want to know who he is. How he came to be searching for me. And why *me* to begin with? He's not human. I've never seen his kind before. I have no clue how *he* was sent to search for survivors and not the guards from the Upper Levels.

Maybe he was hired by New Earth government?

I sniffle some more and try to calm the sobs that are now racking my frame, but as I try to form words, I'm suddenly pulled into a hard chest.

The Atari pulls me into a tight embrace, pressing me into him and absorbing my sobs into his frame. It is so sudden that I freeze, my eyes widening. It only makes my tears come harder and silently, as if his comfort engages with my vulnerability and he's the strength I needed to allow myself to *feel*.

My hands form fists against his chest, my fingers scraping against his skin. But he doesn't even flinch.

"Di-did the president send you?" I manage.

"Not your leaders. Mine. The crown of Atar. They sent us to accept the gift from Earthkin. Females. Potential brides for my people."

I sniffle again. "What?"

"I am aware you know nothing of this. We have already found one female and...she informed us none of the Earthkin on that ship knew they were to be Atari mates."

I freeze, wiping my eyes as I force my breathing to calm. "The cruise..."

"Was not a cruise. Your leaders lied to you, my *ari*. You were meant for *me*." He releases a slow breath. "For *us*." He corrects himself, his jaw ticking. "Your ship was to be hauled back to Atar."

I digest his words and turn them over in my mind. There's no indication he's lying. In fact, everything he's said so solemnly only sounds like the truth...even the parts about me and those other women being a *bridal* gift.

What the...*hell*?

I sniffle again, wiping my nose with my hand, but most of my tears have stopped, so I push away from him slightly, still in his embrace but enough that I can look up at him.

My eyes meet his golden ones immediately and I'm almost struck silent by the pain there. It almost seems tangible, that pain. As if he can understand exactly how I am feeling.

It hits me then, that if what he's saying is true, he entered that club, surrounded by enemies, for *me*. And I have not once inquired if he's alright.

"W-were you hurt?" I ask.

There's a flicker in his gaze. He *is* in pain.

"If it's a minor wound, I can take a look at it," I continue. "I used to patch up my mother after..."

After her lovers would hurt her...taking the frustrations they couldn't express on the Upper Levels out on her as if she were a punching bag.

That memory sobers me completely.

But the Atari's gaze warms, as if my asking is a gift to him. "I am well, my ari. It is *you* who has been hurt."

I release a breath, a soft laugh huffing through my nose as my gaze falls to his chest. "Nothing you could have done about that."

He makes a sound in his throat, a whimper of sorts. One that makes something tingle in my belly.

"My name is Trudy, by the way," I say, my gaze flicking to his once more. "What should I call you?"

"Qhenno," he says.

"Qhenno," I repeat, another tingle going through me that seems to transfer to him because a shiver goes through his chest the same moment his name leaves my lips.

"So...you *did* come for me," I whisper.

Qhenno takes a deep breath and my scalp prickles as he dips his fingers into my hair, combing through the strands, his gaze locked on the movement of the tendrils across his fingers.

"I have been searching for so long..." he whispers. The way he says it makes a little shiver go through me and I dip my forehead to his chest, accepting the comfort he is offering. That sweet fresh scent of his wafts into my nose, making me breathe in deeply and calming me even more.

"If what you're saying is true...it means we were both tricked..." I say.

And it means he's come after me not knowing all the details.

Qhenno makes a soft sound in his throat, one that almost sounds like a "hmm."

"I mean...when we went on that cruise...we thought we were being treated like human beings for once in our lives...and you...your people thought you were getting females for mates."

When his fingers brush against my scalp once more, my eyes almost roll back with how good it feels.

A little voice in my head tells me to pull away. That I shouldn't be accepting comfort from a male that's still a stranger, despite who he says he is. But, for once in my life, I'm too tired to listen.

For once, I just want to...breathe.

"We were not tricked," he says, responding to my previous statement.

I scoff. "Oh, you were. All of us on that ship were from the Lower

Levels. Most of us didn't have licenses to breed or form marriage unions."

His fingers pause only slightly before continuing their rhythmic stroke across my scalp. I lean into him more, turning my cheek to rest against his warm chest.

He feels so good. Too good.

Maybe it's the reality of being down in this cold dark pit, the constant sound of picks meeting rock echoing all around us that I'm trying to hide away from.

Qhenno is the opposite of everything in this place. His golden eyes are like the warmth of the sun. His skin radiates the same heat…

Maybe that's why I'm drawn to him, despite my reservations telling me to be careful. Maybe that's why I'm cuddling up with a stranger, an alien I just met, and feeling, for the first time in my life, a sense of…calm.

"We know about the illegal implants," he says, probably in response to my last statement. It takes me a few moments to recognize what he's talking about.

"Oh, you mean the contraceptive implants? New Earth mandates their use if they deem our DNA unfit. Those?"

I'm surprised he knows about that. My brows rise as does my gaze. I'm greeted by the sharp line of his jaw. He is sculpted like no one I've ever seen before.

"Yes. We will have to get yours removed. It is illegal technology." He pauses. "If your mate marks you…he could kill you."

I release a laugh through my nose and smile, trying to hide the pain I know lingers behind my eyes.

"I don't have an implant. My…legs…they…I wasn't born this way." A lump rises in my throat that I have to force down. Things almost feel…normal. The last thing I want this strange male to do is fixate on my legs when he hasn't seemed to notice them yet.

Even humans on Lower Earth fixate on them as if I'm some strange thing to be stared at, coddled, or even ignored.

I want to keep this serenity in my being for as long as I can. So I huff another laugh through my nose and talk quickly.

"Your species...the mates you find..." I trail off, remembering the Morang boss making that quip about the Atari's fertility problem.

"The fates choose our mates," he replies, that deep voice settling over me like a warm cloak.

Another laugh releases through my nose.

"So you believe in destiny then? Fate?"

"It is what guides us," he replies, his fingers still stroking through my hair like it's a thing he's always done.

"I don't think so."

His fingers pause at my words, and I feel I should continue.

"Not when it's given some of us such a shitty deal."

He makes that sound in his throat again. One that sounds like a "hmm" before he strokes my hair again.

"And what deal have you gotten from the fates, my ari?"

I swallow past the lump in my throat as moments pass between us. I don't know this male. I shouldn't tell him my life story.

But...

My tongue moves before I can stop myself, as if something about this male is a safe space I can dive into.

"I was five when the Upper Level guards killed my father for *allegedly* stealing some rich woman's credits. That left me and my mother alone." I take a breath, the memories soaked in years of pain making it hard to continue. But the alien holding me doesn't press or force me to go on. And somehow, it makes me want to tell him more. "Ma had fibromyalgia. You probably don't know what that is. The Upper Levels have advancements enough that the people there don't suffer from anything, so I don't doubt the technology of your world is even better." When he doesn't interrupt and simply continues stroking his hand through my hair, I continue. "Ma's illness was something my parents managed with both their salaries. With Pa gone and me to feed, she put me first and cut back on her medication." Another lump forms in my throat as the painful memories resurface, and I have to push past it.

Should I stop here? I've never told anyone about this before. On the Lower Levels, moaning to people who all have similar trials as you do isn't done.

Yet, this Atari…someone who can't possibly understand the world I come from…his presence…it's…comforting…

"You probably don't want to hear all this…" I say, ready to ease off him and return to sitting across from him.

He makes that sound in his throat again and the motion of his fingers doesn't pause in my hair.

"Speak, my ari. I am here to listen."

I gulp, his words making something deep inside me tingle.

"What happened to your mor?" he asks.

"I…she…" I take a breath and close my eyes. If this stranger is willing to give me this comfort for but a moment in this nightmare we're trapped in…I should take it. "I remember watching her… watching her suffer and not being able to do anything about it. She couldn't afford her medication and she couldn't afford me. If she could have just held on for a little longer…I was turning sixteen and had a chance to go to the Upper Levels in the yearly intake."

"Intake?"

I nod against his chest. "Yes. The Committee comes to the Lower Levels. You do a health and DNA scan. If you are fit to work and live on the Upper Levels, you do a test. If you pass, your whole life can change. You can become an Upper Level citizen."

Qhenno grunts and I can almost feel his frown.

"I guess something like that is strange to you, huh?"

"There are no levels on Atar. Our people live as one. Everyone has access to what they need."

Must be paradise, I think. But I don't want to say it and sound bitter, for bitterness is the farthest thing from my mind. His world sounds like a dream. A *gift*.

I take another breath. "I was a young, healthy female who could get a good Upper Level job and help my Ma. I was sure I could pass that test. It's just an intelligence test, and I'd been studying for years. But I lost that chance. I…made a stupid mistake."

My words trail off, only the sound of the picks hitting rock and the occasional cough within the mine filters inside the alcove.

"You had an accident…" he says after a few moments, and I can feel his gaze on my legs.

"I slipped off a ledge… A hover car broke my fall…and my spine." I huff a sad laugh through my nose. "Now here I am. So…no, I don't believe in fate and I bet those slaves outside don't believe in it either. No one is destined for shit like this."

There is a slight pause where his hand freezes in my hair and I ease off him, thinking this moment, whatever it was between us, has passed.

But when I look at him, those golden eyes hold so much warmth and feeling, I'm entranced by them. I stare at him, this stranger who has made me open up more than anyone on Lower Earth has done in the seventeen years since my mother passed…and I feel…acknowledged. Valid.

"I am sorry you have suffered so much, my ari," he says after a few moments.

Ari…whatever that means.

Every time he calls me that name, I feel like a flower opening her petals in the sunshine.

I force a smile across my lips, my cheeks flushing when his gaze becomes too intense, too focused.

"Well, now you know," I whisper. "That's my story. They did not force me to have an implant like some of the other women who were on that ship. But…it doesn't matter, anyway."

"Why is that, my *ari*?"

"Because…I don't want a mate."

He stiffens…or at least I think he does.

I guess it sounds strange to him, coming from a world where mates and life bonds are a thing.

But the last thing I want is for someone to feel like they're tied down by me. I've tried dating before…

Over time I've learned, it's better for me to be alone.

8

Qhenno

I stare down at Trudy's dark-brown tendrils, my world stopping and freezing over.

She...doesn't want a mate?

Something twists deep inside my chest, my life organ, as if it has lost the will to continue beating and I have to force myself to breathe.

She doesn't want a mate.

*That means...she doesn't want...**me**.*

I haven't told her she is my ari. My mate. The very being I have dreamed about for many moons. That just by touching her, I can feel life spirit swelling in my fangs. That the urge to tilt her head back and bury them into the soft skin of her neck, marking her as mine forever, is so overpowering, only the fact that she is hurting is forcing my mind to stay clear.

"You don't...want a mate?" My voice is rough, the art of speaking once more seemingly difficult.

She shakes her head, a smile twisting her soft lips. "I do better on my own."

"What if you already have a mate?"

She seems to freeze in my grasp and time ticks between us as if it has nowhere to go.

"Humans don't have mates," she whispers, so low, I almost don't hear it.

"But Atari do..."

There's a clang not far outside the alcove, and some commotion ensues. This little sense of calm and peace we've had together will end soon.

But as I wait for Trudy to respond, it's clear that she won't. She's gone silent, her eyes focused on the alcove's entrance and the darkness that lies beyond it. Her gaze going unreadable as the walls that fell between us rebuild.

This little space in time, where we are no longer strangers but just two beings sharing a moment, is ending.

When a Morang pops his head inside the alcove, she doesn't even jerk in surprise.

A growl rumbles in my throat at the sight of him, and I sit up straighter, still holding Trudy tucked into my chest.

The Morang's dark eyes flick from her to me before he snickers, his sharp teeth coming into view. "Time for fekking is up, Atari. Get to work!"

I watch him sneer as he takes a few more seconds to look at us, his gaze passing between me and my mate, before he finally pulls away. It is at that moment that Trudy moves, bracing against my chest, her cold fingers like ice against my skin as she tries to leave the comfort of my embrace.

"We should go," she whispers. "It will take a while to find even one gem." She lets out a sad sort of chuckle. "For a moment there, I almost forgot where I was."

When I don't immediately release her, she looks up at me. There's a strange sort of look in her eyes, one I can't decipher. One filled with pain, sadness, and something else.

"I know you probably don't want to do this..." she says. "But if we don't, they'll throw us over the edge of the platform. I've seen them do it before." Her shoulders heave. "And...the last thing I want is someone else's death on my shoulders." She sighs, her voice lowering till it's almost inaudible. "The only reason you're here is because of me."

With that, she gives me a tight smile. One that only thins her lips and doesn't show her teeth.

It is more like a grimace than anything else.

That brings me back to the order of the moment.

"This is not how I wanted to meet you…not how it should have been…" I say the words to myself, but Trudy pauses, that strange look intensifying in her eyes. I lower my voice, careful to not let it filter outside the alcove. "What if I tell you I have a plan? A way to get us out of this."

It is almost as if I feel her life organ give a sudden thump, or maybe it is just the fates binding us together. There is a sudden light in her eyes that wasn't there just a moment before. That same look, hope, that I'd seen die in her eyes…it returns, flaring to life and bleeding into her gaze.

"A plan?" she whispers, her eyes darting to the alcove's entrance.

"Yes…" I say to her, "but I must ask you to do one thing."

She licks her lips, nodding her head immediately. "Anything."

"Put your trust in me."

***

Trudy

I grip on to Qhenno's broad shoulders as he rises with me still in his arms, my eyes widening at the movement.

"Y-you don't have to carry me everywhere." My whisper is harsh, but he doesn't even blink.

"I will not let you crawl. I am not like those brutes called the Morang." There's a growl in his voice, one that makes my insides suddenly turn into jelly and something quiver in between my legs.

He seems so sweet when he's talking to me, but at even the slightest hint or mention of a Morang, he becomes deadly.

A blush creeps across my cheeks the moment he exits the alcove, and I can feel the other slaves watching us. Funny, I didn't even notice them when we first arrived. Now though, their gazes only make every bit of my body that's touching Qhenno heat like I'm on a stove.

I clear my throat and try to focus on everything else except him. But that is hard, especially when he crouches in between two slaves and readjusts me in his arms so I'm promptly straddling him.

The heat in my cheeks could warm the entire mine shaft and all the alcoves along with it.

"What are you doing?!" My voice is hardly a whisper with the silence around us. Every male, female, and other being is looking at us right now.

"Get back to work!" a Morang shouts from somewhere above and the clangs of picks hitting rock begin again shortly after.

"What are you doing?" I whisper again, careful to keep my voice low. "I can't work if I'm…" I glance between us, my throat growing dry, "If I'm sitting like *this*."

Straddling you…my crotch pressed against your belly…only the thin cloth of my cotton pants between us.

Gods help me…

When did I go from thinking he's a possible asshole to sitting on him like I'm about to ride his cock?

Qhenno grunts and I see a ghost of a smile as he looks down at me.

"Did you think I would let you work? Your impression of me is disappointing, my ari."

I blink at him. What the hell is he talking about? "I *have* to work."

He shakes his head. "Never again, and especially not when I'm around."

With that, he grabs a pick and slams it into the rock behind me. I jerk at the suddenness of it and Qhenno uses his free hand to pull me closer to him and shield me.

I have no option but to wrap my arms around his neck.

It's either that or have them crushed awkwardly between us.

Trying to calm the sudden irregular beats of my heart, my wide eyes land on the slave next to us—that light-blue male who had been working by my side when they'd stationed me higher on this rickety platform.

He stares at me as if I am suddenly a stranger and my cheeks heat even more.

"Qhenno," I whisper, "people are watching us."

He rumbles in his throat, and it vibrates against my chest. When he slams the pick into the wall once more, his whole body moves against mine.

Like a battery that needed charging, a throb goes through me, right down to my center.

"Let them watch," he says, a laugh on the edge of his voice.

I ease back a little to stare at him.

Is there something in the air out here that makes him go crazy?

Is there something in the air that's making *me* go crazy?

"Is this what you had in mind when you said you have a plan?" I whisper, pressing my mouth into a thin line when he slams the pick into the wall once more and my whole body responds to the friction it causes between us.

"Negative," he replies, and it is then that I realize his gaze remains high above us as he works. I look up and spot the Morang he is watching.

The brute sneers at us, cracking his whip on an unsuspecting slave out of spite.

I wince and pull my gaze away, my heart beating hard.

But the Morang says nothing about the fact I am in Qhenno's arms and not abusing the rock with a pick.

As Qhenno slams his pick into the wall again, I try not to feel self-conscious that I'm straddling him, this handsome alien male, as if he's mine.

That thought makes another one of those strange feelings settle in my chest, and I swallow the lump that's forming in my throat.

"What if you already have a mate?"
"Humans don't have mates."
"But Atari do..."

Memory of his words only intensifies the strange feeling in my chest.

I don't want to assume, and I was too afraid to ask what he meant by that…because it almost felt like…he was saying there's *more* to him being here.

More to his strange urge to protect me—a human he knows nothing about.

As I force down another swallow, that lump in my throat doesn't budge. A tentative lift of my head and I note Qhenno isn't even looking at the rock wall before him. He's scanning the platforms above, his gaze lingering when he spots a Morang.

What is he planning?

If it involves fighting, I should be prepared.

I might not be good on my feet, but I can be mean with my hands.

The more he watches them, the more excitement thrums in my veins. Hope flares within me that there might actually be a chance out of this mess. My adrenaline rises, and it is a conscious effort to keep my breathing steady.

To my right, the familiar light-blue alien eyes us, his head tilted down as he sends covert glances our way. His gaze flicks to how my arms grasp Qhenno's shoulders, then to my legs and how Qhenno's wrapped them around his waist.

His gaze darts to my face and he looks away.

I open my mouth to say something to him when he suddenly turns to me fully, his gaze darting above us as he checks if a Morang is close by.

"Did you see Tilly?" he asks.

My brow furrows slightly. "Tilly?"

"The Neturi female the Morang took along with you when you were brought above."

"Neturi…" I frown. I don't know what he means.

"She is small…smaller than you. Skin like the soft sands of Kamar…"

Understanding dawns, even though I don't know the planet he speaks of.

"Oh, you mean the nymph?" My eyes dart above as well, as I check if any Morang are watching us.

They don't like to see the slaves speaking to each other. Probably afraid of us forming alliances and turning against them. That fact makes it even stranger that they allow Qhenno to hold me like this.

"Nymph?" the light-blue male asks.

"She helped me," I say, my eyes darting back to him. "She helped me while I was up there."

A ghost of a smile passes over his lips but it doesn't dim the worry in her eyes. "Please," he says, "if you leave this place, take her with you. She is my mate. Her life means more to me than my own."

My eyes widen slightly as I stare at his pleading ones.

"I..."

How can I promise to do such a thing when I don't even know how I'm going to get *myself* out of this situation?

"Aye," Qhenno says, and it is only then that I realize he was listening in. "Do not fret, Cambrian. You will see your mate again."

The light-blue male's throat moves, some hope flaring in his gaze right before a Morang shouts from above. A whip cracks and some poor slaves cry out in distress.

Turning back to the rock, the Cambrian slams his pick in with force, his chin dipping to his chest in acknowledgment to me as he continues to work.

Picks hit rock, over and over, drowning out the sound of the slave whimpering somewhere above us as everyone doubles down on working.

Qhenno's body sways as he leans forward and back, driving the pick into the rock with more force than I could have ever mustered.

Glancing over my shoulder, I see that he's made a hole that would have taken me at least three days to make on my own and my brows shoot up in surprise.

Across his chest, a thin sheet of perspiration forms. He's still so warm, even in this cold cavern.

"There," he suddenly says and the Cambrian male beside us looks our way, his eyes bugging out.

"How did he—" he begins.

Turning to look at what he's seen, my eyes bug out too.

Qhenno eases forward, his fingers collecting not one, but two, three, no *four* gems.

"How did you…" I whisper.

"The fates," he whispers, his breath brushing against my ear.

A delicious shiver runs down to my center.

Taking two of the gems, he gives one each to the slaves on either side of us, making their mouths fall open as he rises with me in his arms.

"Wait, that's it?" I ask, my eyes widening. "We're done?" I can't believe I'm asking that. As if I want to stay out here and work more.

"Yes, my ari," Qhenno says, moving into the alcove once more. He places the gems in my palm after he sets me down, and closes my hand over them.

"Keep these with you," he says, his gaze darting back outside to the center of the shaft. "If those scum come to check if we have met their quota for the cycle, you show them these."

I shake my head, information coming into my brain too quickly. "Wait, you're leaving?"

"Not leaving…but I must scout what I can before I make my move…" He reaches forward, his fingers brushing into my hair and, for a moment, he pauses, staring down at me.

And then he slips away.

I watch him go, my eyes wide, my mouth open.

He found four gems, two for us and two for the slaves working beside us. No one in this cavern is insane enough to give away their gems—except for me and now him. Even as he disappears from the alcove's entrance and I can no longer see him, I can hear the whispers traveling up the platform of what he's done.

For the first time since being in this mine, I don't have to drag myself to my station and work until my fingers bleed.

For the first time, I have time to think…and the only thing on my mind is the Atari who has crashed into my life and is shattering everything I know.

9

Trudy

I'm alone in the alcove for long enough that when a shadow appears at the entrance, I sit upright, a smile coming to my lips that instantly freezes and becomes stiff.

I thought Qhenno had returned…but it isn't his face that pops in.

It's the face of that conniving green male that had been stationed beside me when I was placed higher along the platform.

I stiffen immediately. What is *he* doing here?

The Cambrian male, still at his station outside, says something to him that I cannot hear. Something he ignores, his gaze flicking upward and along the platform above him before he pierces me with those cold eyes of his.

"What do you want?" I ask. I stiffen as his gaze flicks around the small alcove. *What is he looking for?*

"Where are they?" he asks, pushing himself halfway into the alcove. My whole body freezes, the hairs along my arm and neck rising as my senses tingle, and I grip the gems still in my palm even tighter.

"Where are *what*?" I pretend I don't know what he's asking for, but he could only be looking for one thing. "If you had something in this alcove, it was gone before they put me here."

"Stupid female," he growls, moving closer. His gaze flicks over me before landing on my fists in my lap. My heart skips a beat, and not in a good way. "Give me the gems."

"What *gems*?" I can almost feel my clavicle standing out with the way my neck's stiff. He's a bully. I was right not to trust him before.

"The ones your mate gave away freely," he snarls. "You give the Cambrian and you give none to me, after I have protected you while you worked above."

My face scrunches with shock at how ridiculous his statement is. "What?!"

Protected me? When? He must think I'm a fool to suggest that him not attacking me all those nights was him "protecting" me.

The Cambrian reaches in and grabs the green dude's shoulder. "Leave the female," he says. "You can have the gem her mate gave me, if you wish. I will work to find another."

I'm about to say Qhenno's not my mate when the green alien growls loudly, pushing the Cambrian so hard he stumbles backward, narrowly missing the edge of the platform.

My eyes widen, my heart thumping hard as every single one of my senses tells me I am in danger.

"Stay away from me," I warn him, putting my hands behind my back. If he thinks I'll just give him the gems Qhenno worked so hard to find for us, he is as wrong as snow in the summer. "You want gems, go and work for them like everybody else in this godforsaken pit!"

My words make such rage grow in his eyes that I see it clear as day. He climbs into the alcove and grabs me by the shoulder, his fingers digging into my skin so hard that I cry out.

I try to shrug him off, but can't. He's too strong, and when a swift blow connects with my jaw, my vision wanes and comes back before waning again.

Distantly, I can taste blood in my mouth as my ears ring.

My head lolls as he pries the gems from my hand and even though I try to grip them, it's of no use. There's too much pounding in my head and my arms feel weak.

The moment he gets the gems is the moment he shuffles away. Through blurred vision, I see the victorious sneer on his face as he exits and my hatred for him almost gains its own persona.

And then he's gone…

The gems…I lost our gems…

All I see is the blurry outline of someone else as they enter the alcove.

"Qhenno?"

I say his name as if it comes naturally. As if I've always called out to him. But it isn't him that enters. It is the Cambrian, his eyes wide.

His hand hovers over my jaw.

"I will fetch your mate," he says.

"He isn't my…" But he's already moving.

I reach for my jaw and just touching it sends pain through my skull. Squeezing my eyes tight, I force the dizziness away.

I do not need a concussion. Not now.

It must have been minutes, but it feels much faster than that when the dim light is blocked by another figure.

"Qhenno?" I breathe, placing my hand on my jaw as I stretch it and wince.

"Trudy?" There's shuffling as Qhenno climbs inside. His voice is strained and when he gently pries my hand away from my jaw, he freezes.

"I lost our gems," I mutter, my lips thinning into a line.

Maybe my vision is still blurry, or my eyes have been affected by that punch, but the look on Qhenno's face would send a chill down my spine if I wasn't so preoccupied with the pain in my skull.

His face is a mask…one of cold, cold ice.

His gaze bleeds to black as he stares at me, his jaw clenching and his throat working.

"Who did this to you?"

He cradles my cheek gently, a complete contrast to the look on his face.

He looks like a demon and I should be afraid. God knows I should be afraid. Why am I not afraid?

"He wanted the gems…" I trail off.

I need a knife. If I had one, I would have gutted that asshole before he could steal from me. But I was empty-handed.

The only ones with weapons in this place are the Morang.

My jaw aches with the bruise and I try not to talk, only wincing as I try to keep still.

Qhenno's hand trembles against my skin before he suddenly disappears, climbing out of the alcove so quickly it's like he wasn't just before me.

"Qhenno?"

There's movement on the platform from the way it shakes, and I hear some slaves exclaim.

It takes a lot more effort than usual to move toward the alcove's entrance and when I get there, the sight that greets my eyes has me simply staring transfixed.

Qhenno moves up the platform with what looks like murderous intent. He might not have seen the green male steal our gems but he doesn't even stop to ask any of the other slaves if they're the ones that did it. And that's probably because they are all pointing upward, their eyes wide and filled with fear as they gaze at him.

I've only seen them look at the Morang like that.

But Qhenno looks like a force to be reckoned with.

His fangs have extended, his fingernails elongated into claws, and he looks impossibly larger. As he climbs the platform, it becomes difficult to see. Everyone is as transfixed as I am and when he stops walking, I can hear his voice ring through the mine shaft.

"You."

Fuck. That one word sounds uttered not by a man but by something otherworldly. He's pissed, and everyone in the entire mine can hear it.

"He found him," the Cambrian says, suddenly appearing by my side. "Qef...he's Atari. That fool didn't realize your mate is Atari?"

My mate...?

I swallow those words as my gaze searches the platform above, worry making my heart beat faster.

"Where are the Morang?" I whisper, and the Cambrian shrugs.

Qhenno disappears from view as he steps closer to the wall of the shaft, but his voice rings out loud and clear since everyone seems to have stopped working to listen. "You touched her," he growls. "*My female. You put your hands on her…*"

His female…?

"You're *Atari?*" I recognize the sleazebag's voice immediately, and for the first time, I hear what it sounds like when he is afraid.

"*Surprise,*" Qhenno says, his voice filled with only the calmness death offers.

"You can have the gems back." The scumbag must have thrown them at Qhenno because there's a distinct clink as they hit the platform and fall over the side, disappearing into the abyss. There are a few gasps as they disappear into the darkness.

Those gems mean food. Safety. And now they are gone.

There's a beat of silence and I wonder what Qhenno will do before there is suddenly a roar. It rings so loudly, echoing against the rock walls, I wonder if the whole mine shaft will collapse on top of us.

And then I hear it, the distinct sound of a fist hitting flesh.

"Qhenno!" I scream his name. If he gets hurt…

If he gets hurt, what? When did I begin to care about him so much?

There's a grunt and a muffled scream as a male whines, whimpers, and begs for mercy.

"*Apologize,*" Qhenno growls. "Loud enough that she can hear you, you *scum.*"

"I—I regret—"

Qhenno cuts him off. "Your apology means *nothing.*"

There's the sound of another punch before I see the dude dangling off the side of the platform. There are gasps, loud ones, as everyone holds their breath, including me.

My eyes widen as Qhenno holds the male over the abyss with only one arm. "I should beat you till *you beg to die,*" he says. "*How weak can you be to put your hands on a female?*"

"Atari!" The sound of the Morang guards breaks the silence Qhenno's words created. "Cease."

Qhenno ignores them. "*I am not yet satisfied,*" he snarls.

I gulp, something warming inside me that really shouldn't. I should be horrified. This shouldn't be making warmth settle in my gut. I shouldn't be feeling a sense of justice being served…should I?

"Release the slave!" the Morang order, two racing toward Qhenno from either side. Had they just been watching all along?

Qhenno growls. "Gladly."

The world stutters for a moment as the male falls, the abyss swallowing him like a hungry monster as he screams. My heart thumps, my eyes wide as I stare down into the darkness.

No one moves. Even the Morang seem surprised, and when Qhenno brushes past them, heading back in my direction, they don't even stop him.

He walks with an air of authority, and many of the slaves' gazes find me. They dip their heads once I lock eyes with them, an unsaid message passing among them all.

Fuck with her and get killed.

My heart thumps harder as Qhenno approaches and beside me, the Cambrian snorts. "Serve him right," he says, before returning to his station.

I watch the Atari warrior head back toward me, eyes still as black as night, blood on his fists, and it is clear he is no slave like the rest of us.

Even the Morang know that.

But what is he to me?

10

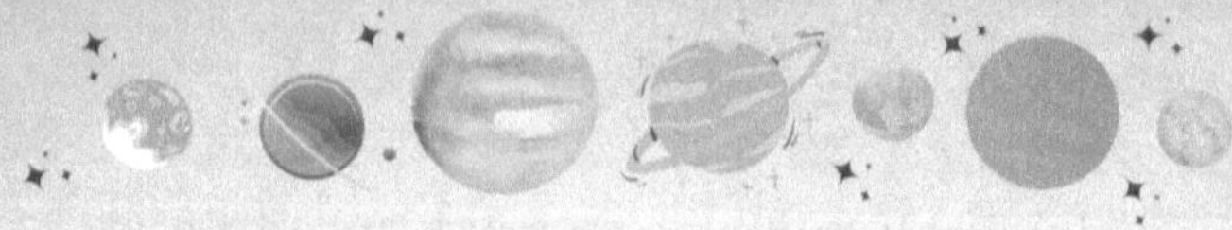

Qhenno

Some slave brought me water I didn't ask for. I accepted it anyway, cleaning my hands of that vermin's lifeblood.

I can sense their gazes, the covert glances as I rid my skin of the scum and turn toward the alcove.

Trudy is at the entrance, all wide eyes as she waits for me.

It is a conscious effort not to look at her and growl, for every time I look her way, I see that mark on her jaw.

That pile of excrement…

I hope he dies before he meets what's at the bottom of this hole.

"Come, my ari," I say to Trudy as I turn toward the alcove. Her gaze is full of questions as I move toward her, pull her into my arms, and crawl with her into the depths of the small space.

"Are you alright?" she whispers, her eyes searching mine.

I'm so qeffed up in the head, I don't know whether my gaze is still bled to black or if my eyes are back to their regular gold.

The fury that consumed me seeing that mark on her face, the fury consuming me *now* as I stare at it.

I growl without realizing and I'm surprised when Trudy doesn't quail or try to pull away from me.

She lifts a hand and brushes it against her bruised skin. "It's not so bad now. The pain's mostly gone."

My nostrils flare with barely concealed rage. "He had no right to enter your space. Worse, to lay his filthy hands on you."

She dips her head and I can tell she is thinking.

"You threw him over the edge..."

"Believe me, my ari, he is lucky that is what I did. I wanted to tear him apart."

She startles a little, wide eyes turned up to me and I wonder if I have said too much. But there is still no fear in her gaze.

There's a sound at the alcove's entrance and I turn with a growl to see who has dared to disturb my mate's sleeping place once more.

A small Usippi male stands there, his hands outstretched and trembling.

"Please accept this balm," he says.

My brows dive and he hurries on, his tall ears folding forward. "For ridding us of that pest. He has stolen gems from many before and caused them to be thrown off the platform," he says, his ears folding even more. "Two moons ago, he stole from my mor. Before we could replace what he took, the Morang threw her into the abyss."

I am not surprised, but I hear Trudy's soft gasp. Qeffers like that scum prey on the weak.

My gaze falls to the Usippi's hands and he thrusts them toward me. They are dirty, but within his palms there is a green fluid.

"Made with my own fangs, oh great warrior. It will soothe your mate's wound, help it heal."

My gaze flicks back to his face and I study him. Usippi can produce two sets of fluid in their fangs. One is poisonous. The other has healing properties.

He wouldn't dare harm Trudy, not after what I just did. He knows I will kill him if he tries. So I nod and accept his healing balm into my palm, staring at it as he shuffles away hurriedly.

Trudy sniffs, her nose wrinkling in a way that's lovable enough to make me stare at it.

"Smells like vegetable oil," she says.

I dip my nose to my palm and sniff. I can't smell a thing.

"Give it a try," she says.

I wait, studying her some more. "You trust him?"

She shakes her head immediately. "No…but I trust you."

I can only gaze at her.

Does she have any clue what she just said?

She trusts me.

I could not have asked for more.

A beat passes between us as Trudy smiles up at me, and I am suddenly caught in her spell.

In this dark hole, her smile is like the greatest gift.

Shifting, I allow her to brace on her arms as I apply the Usippi's healing balm and watch as it dries on her skin. She isn't like Atari, she will take much longer to heal, but I can tell the balm at least numbs the sting of the bruise.

"You must rest now," I say to her, but she shakes her head.

"We lost the gems. When the Morang come, we will have nothing and I have seen what they do to slaves who are empty-handed."

My jaw ticks. I have not forgotten about the Morang…or how they stood in the shadows and watched while that poor excuse for a male placed his hands on my mate.

"Do not fret…" I tell her. "I will take care of it."

She gazes at me for a moment before nodding. "Okay."

My life organ swells and thumps hard. She *does* trust me.

"Rest now."

I shift, pulling her on top of me as I rest against the cold rock. I hear when she begins to protest but a purr in my chest causes her words to trail off.

This will be our first night together and I try not to mourn the plans of grandeur I'd dreamt up in those days when I never had a mate. Of a spotless nest filled with things that my mate holds dear and of how I would spread warm oils over her skin, stimulating her body till she whimpered and cried for me to sink deep inside her.

Reaching for my tunic, I spread it on top of her and pull her even closer.

It is hardly a suitable covering, but it will do for now.
She will not have to stay in this hole for much longer.

11

My eyes flicker open to darkness and I frown.

I slept? So soundly?

Soundly enough for me to know a lot of time has passed because my body feels…rested.

It must be morning…or whatever passes for morning in this dark hole. Time is easy to forget with the constant sound of picks hitting rock, never ceasing, even when you try to sleep.

I groan and stretch my arms, my skin rubbing against warm velvet that suddenly makes me start.

"Qhenno!"

I jerk against him and his arms immediately circle me.

Did he keep me on top of him all night? No wonder I feel like I've had the best sleep I've ever had since being in this hole.

"My ari," he drawls, his voice having a hoarseness to it that's thick with sleep. "You awaken."

I try to sit upright and give him some relief from having borne my weight all night, but he holds me tighter.

"How is your jaw?"

I stretch my jaw, opening my mouth wide and closing it. Surprisingly, the sting isn't there.

"It doesn't hurt anymore."

Qhenno makes a comforting sound in his chest that makes warmth spread all over me.

"The healing fluid will work for a little while longer," he says, "but do not fret, I will see that you attend a med bay as soon as we leave this place."

As I'm forced to stay on top of him, the thought that I might actually find a way out of here is stronger than it ever was before.

Yet, even with that possibility now in front of me, I can't seem to focus on the fact. All I can think about is the feel of the male underneath me, how he's holding me close, and everything he's done for me so far.

When I first laid eyes on him, I didn't know what to think. And now, I'm even more confused about his presence here.

"Qhenno..." I whisper, and his head tilts forward, his chin brushing into my hair at the sound of his name. He rubs his jaw against the top of my head in a way that renders me silent for a moment, as I forget what I'd called his name for.

"Yes, my ari?" he says after a few moments.

Clearing my throat, I force myself to focus on the darkness outside the alcove. "I want to ask you something..."

"Anything," he replies.

Fuck, I might as well just ask.

"Earlier...what did you mean—"

High above us, a commotion begins and I can hear the platform shaking as the Morang guards hurry toward whatever dispute is occurring.

Qhenno ignores the sound and rubs his face into my hair before burying his nose into it.

I clear my throat and continue. "Earlier, when I said humans don't have mates. You said 'but Atari do'...what did you mean by that?"

I wonder if I am reading too much into things, but my throat is tight as I wait for his answer.

Everyone thinks he's my mate...what if...

Surely, that's not what he thinks too.

"Atari have mates," he says after a few moments. "But some are luckier than others. Some have already found their mates. Some are left endlessly searching for theirs."

There's a note of sadness there, one I'm not sure I should unpack. But I push on anyway.

"Have you found yours? Your mate, I mean."

"I have…" he says after a few moments.

I gulp. "Ok, last question." And possibly the most important one.

As I open my mouth to ask, there's a growl that sounds like it's directed right at us.

"*You*, Atari." The Morang at the front of the alcove almost makes me jump out of my skin.

Qhenno growls back as a Morang leans inside.

"The boss requests your presence," the Morang says, the words coming from his mouth as if he despises having to utter them.

Qhenno stiffens and I can already tell he is not about to go. I don't want him to go either.

"*Without* the female," the Morang adds.

I swear Qhenno growls again. "She goes where I go."

"Not unless you wish to be separated," the Morang sneers. "We can move her to another mine if you refuse to cooperate."

That's the only time that Qhenno actually moves. Holding me against him, he rises into a sitting position and I fall into his lap.

I gulp, watching the Morang as his cold gaze pierces us.

Qhenno stares right back, meeting that coldness with ice of his own.

But the Morang's right. They could move me to another mine…and there's not much I could do about it.

"I'll be fine," I turn to Qhenno. After what he did yesterday, I doubt anyone will dare to even approach me.

He stares at me, his gaze unreadable, before he slowly shifts and sets me down.

"Make it quick," he growls at the Morang as he crawls from the alcove.

Once outside, he dips his head to look at me, unsaid words communicated in that golden gaze.

A promise that he will return.

I nod.

Fuck...I don't know what's happening to me, but my heart begins beating at an unsteady pace as soon as he disappears and I'm left alone. Pulling his tunic to my chest, I dip my head into it and inhale deeply.

I swallow hard, an unfamiliar feeling twisting my gut and I grip his tunic even tighter.

If they harm him...

I stare down at the tunic. If they harm him, what? He's still a stranger. Only a heroic one that stuck his neck out for you more than once... Only a god that makes your insides quiver... A male that makes your silly heart hope for something you could previously only dream of...

Gulping down the worrisome feeling growing in my gut, I fold Qhenno's tunic and set it down at the head of the alcove.

We lost our gems yesterday. I should try to find us some more. At least until he returns and starts putting whatever plan he has in motion.

As I exit the alcove, I feel the other slaves' eyes on me. I guess yesterday still has everyone flustered.

Moving over to my spot beside the Cambrian male, I give him a smile.

He dips his chin to his chest in acknowledgment, his gaze darting upward as he checks for Morang.

"Your mate," he says, his voice low. "What is his plan?"

My eyes widen slightly, the pick stalling in my hand. "His plan?"

How did he know Qhenno has a plan?

"We are all waiting for his signal," the Cambrian whispers. "With a warrior like him on our side, we can overturn the Morang." His whisper grows lower. "I have seen the Atari at war. No one gets between them and their mates."

I blink at him, my mouth opening to tell him I am *not* Qhenno's mate, but the words stall on my tongue.

I can't be…

But how would I know if I was anyway…

Swallowing hard, I turn from the Cambrian and slam my pick into the wall, focusing on the destruction it brings as it splits the rock. It's the only thing I can do for all the thoughts swarming in my head.

I'm so intent on finding those gems that when a rough hand closes on my shoulder, I jump, my arm holding the pick swinging in the attacker's direction.

The Morang guard grabs my wrist as he growls.

I quail.

Why is he here?

Gripping my shoulder harshly, he pulls me upward and I grab on to his hand for some stability.

"I am working to find your gems." I grit my teeth, forcing the words through them. "What do you want?"

The Morang leans in close to me, those sharp teeth displayed. "You use your mouth against me because you think you have power now that your mate is here?"

He's lifted me so high, it is only my grasp on him that gives me some confidence that if he lets me go, I won't just fall to the ground.

"It is no wonder you are going to the cells," he growls, turning with me still in his grasp.

The cells?

My eyes catch the wide ones of the Cambrian male as he stretches an arm toward me. But he can't help. Not without being punished.

I struggle against the Morang's grasp. "Where are you taking me?!"

"Thank your mate for this," is all he growls. "You could have ended your life well here, working and gathering gems. Now you will know real torture."

His words send a chill down my spine but they don't quell my growing fury.

"Qhenno has nothing to do with this. *This is all on you and your despicable species.*"

The Morang spins so fast I get slightly dizzy, and when he thrust me forward, slamming my back into the cold rock wall of the mine shaft, I see stars.

Pain shoots across my back, and I choke.

"You will learn to use that mouth of yours for better things," he growls, thrusting his hips forward, and bile rises in my throat.

"Put her here," another says, and I'm suddenly being thrown from one to another. This one's grasp is just as painful as the other, but it doesn't last long before I'm thrown onto a cold rock floor.

A strong scent of ammonia fills my nostrils as a set of bars slams shut, the metal ringing in my ears.

Panic shoots through me as I crawl toward the bars, a basketball-sized lump swelling in my gut.

No.

It's a cell. One set into one of the alcoves. A small dark hole within the larger one that holds me prisoner. It is even worse than being in the shaft, for in this little space, I'll have no option but to face my desolation.

Rushing to the bars, I grip them and scream at the Morang walking away.

But they laugh. I can see their shoulders shake as they carry on along the platform, and any slaves nearby avert their gazes, the light of hope dying in their eyes even as the thirst for revenge begins in mine.

Where is Qhenno...*and what have they done to him?*

Red-hot fury fills me, pushing past all the uncertainty that has filled my mind up to this point.

They have not kept their word.

My hands tremble on the bars, my whole body shaking as I stare out from this new prison.

And at that moment, I realize one thing.

Since Qhenno's arrival, I have been slowly filled with hope. Hope for tomorrow. Hope for the future. And now, that feeling is seeping away, melding with the darkness that threatens to swallow me whole.

I grab hold of the feeling, unwilling to let it go, and in doing so, I grab on to the thought of *him*.

I don't know where it comes from and I don't question it. I only know that I *must* see Qhenno.

For if they have harmed him, all the gods across a million stars know, even if I die in here, my soul will seek vengeance.

12

Qhenno

The Morang boss sits before me on his raised platform. The revelers in his club now gone, the place is deserted and I wonder if he simply sits here to feel as if he has a kingdom over which he rules.

Behind him, several females stand at his service, and I spot the Neturi the Cambrian asked about. His mate is small, smaller than mine, and just as vulnerable.

I promised him her freedom, and in a few moments, she will get it.

The sensitive skin at the back of my neck pulses as I stare at the Morang boss. An indicator of the danger around me. A sign I should tread carefully.

"Welcome," the Morang says finally, his gaze moving over my form.

I do not return his greeting. We both know this is no amicable meeting. Why play games?

"If this is about the male who used his fist on my mate…"

The Morang boss grins, his sharp teeth coming into view. "That is all behind us."

He rises and I try not to snarl.

"I have a proposition for you, Atari," he says, moving closer.

My eyes narrow and when I do not take his bait, he continues.

"Four gems you found, when your shift had only just begun."

I watch him as he makes a slow circle.

"Luck," I reply.

The Morang tilts his head. "It may be so…but I think you can be an asset in my mines."

We had an agreement…" And even though I have no intention of observing said agreement, he doesn't know that.

He tilts his head both ways, his tongue sliding to move over his lips. "Things change." He watches me, those cold eyes seeing everything. "I sense you are against my proposal even before you hear it…"

My jaw ticks.

This qeffer…

He is playing games, and I am not in the mood.

"The strength of an Atari working in my mine," he continues, circling me slowly. At the four corners of the room, his guards stay stationed, ready to move in if anything should happen.

My nostrils flare. They better keep their eyes open.

"You could mine gems three times as fast as one of those weaklings." The Morang boss stops at my side and the urge to slam my elbow into his snout is almost overpowering.

"That is why I will move you to my mine in the arid lands," he finishes and I growl immediately, turning to face him.

He holds his ground but I can almost smell that slight twinge of fear.

"Careful, Atari," he says. "I did not have to inform you of this…but I thought it best…in case you needed an incentive."

"What…*incentive*…?"

He flicks a hand, stepping away from me as a holo image appears in front of us.

I stare at it, unable to breathe.

She is there. My mate. *Trudy*.

I see as the Morang lifts her from where she sits mining that cursed rock. He grips her so hard, she winces and I can almost feel her pain as if it is my own.

My eyes bleed to black immediately and a growl leaves my chest, trembling the air in the room.

But the scene only gets worse.

He slams her into the rock wall and she cries out. There is no sound on the holo-image, but I can see it. Her mouth moves almost as if she calls my name and something deep inside me twists.

My fangs extend, my claws following as the final image of her being thrown into a cell displays before the projection ends.

I lock eyes with the Morang and his guards approach, flocking him like nizits to sucre.

Fear wafts from them like a drug that makes my fangs thirst for blood. Looking at them, I know they are aware they are about to die.

At the back, the females scurry behind the bar, the tension in the room a clear indicator they need to take cover.

"You *dare*," I say to the Morang.

"It is business," the boss says. "The female will remain in that cell. She will be fed. She will not have to find my gems...as long as you continue to deliver them from the rock to me."

I almost laugh.

I suppose this ruse would end sooner or later. I preferred later, for my mate's sake. But he is forcing me to play my hand.

Standing up straighter, I stretch the muscles in my back.

"I promised her something," I say, and the Morang glances at his guards.

"What?" he asks.

"I promised her something. Granted, she didn't hear me say it out loud, but I remember my promise well."

He glances at his guards again.

"When she was here..." I look at the floor. "*When you had her crawling to serve you.*" There's a growl at the end of my words and the Morang wisely takes a step backward.

"What was your promise?" There's a slight wariness to his words, one that should have been there from the start. *Before he thought to put my mate in a cell.*

"You called her...'broken'..." I say, lifting my gaze to his.

His oily tongue flicks out of his mouth, over his lips, and he takes another step backward. Or maybe I have moved forward, because his guards are much closer to me than before.

"I promised her I would show you what that means."

I smile at him, my fangs showing, and recognition finally fills his eyes.

But it's too late.

Launching myself forward, I grip the first two guards by the neck and slam their heads together, a battle cry roaring from my chest that I'm sure can be heard all the way down to the mine.

The two collapse and I take on the other two, grabbing a spear as it is thrust at me and pulling the Morang forward. With a kick, I bury my foot in his gut and he doubles over.

Pulling the spear from his grasp is easy, and I spin and twist as his comrade charges. He comes too fast, not realizing a spear is in my hand, and I surge into him, allowing him to impale himself on the weapon. He staggers back, releasing the spear he was carrying, and I spin on the Morang boss, just as the two whose craniums I'd slammed together rise.

Taking care of them is quick work. I don't even see them. All I can see is the Morang boss' cold, dark eyes widen as he turns and tries to hurry away.

He bellows out in his mother tongue, calling for reinforcements and I laugh.

It is a cruel sound. One I revel in.

All I can see is Trudy's face as she holds on to those bars…and all I want is their blood. They have wronged her. Made her hurt. Caused her pain.

I catch the Morang boss by the neck and pull him backward.

He spins in my grasp, trying to sink his teeth into my arm, but he is predictable.

I shift and slam him into the floor.

"Lesson one," I growl, gripping his claw and twisting it.

I can hear the bones break under his roar of pain.

"That's *broken*."

But it is not enough.

He must *suffer*. He must *bleed*.

Gripping his skull, I slam it into the floor as I press the tip of the spear into his neck, drawing his lifeblood.

"We can make a new arrangement," he sputters.

I ignore him.

"Lesson two," I say, slamming his head into the floor again. "And learn quickly, because your light will soon die."

Fear enters his gaze like a tangible being but he still makes one last-ditch effort to swipe his good claw at me.

Mistake.

I grab it and break those bones too.

His roars of pain are nothing as I slam his head into the floor. Only when his skull cracks do I stop.

Rising to my feet, I grab the spears from the floor and finish the guards still writhing.

Then and only then do I move over to the bar where the females are hiding.

They startle when they see me, and one begins praying to the gods, begging for her life to be spared.

I drop the extra spears at their feet, holding only one in my grasp.

"Take arms if you wish to follow me." I focus on the small Neturi female. "Your mate wishes to see you again."

She swallows hard, but she is the first to grab a spear and I can hear her small footsteps as she follows behind me.

Any guards I meet on the way are quickly taken care of.

They are foolish to stand in my way.

For I am going to my mate, the one I have craved all this time, and nothing, *no one*, is going to stop me from taking her out of here.

13

Trudy

It's the commotion I hear first. That and then the rushing of feet beating against the platform.

Lifting my head, I look out through the bars, the sight before me causing me to sit up straighter.

Slaves, many of them, too much to count are rushing upward, picks in hand.

I pull myself upright, both hands hanging on to the bars as I stare out into the mine shaft.

Something's happening…

They've never acted like this before.

And it can only be because of him. I'm sure of it.

My heart thumps hard in my chest as I tilt my head, craning my neck to see as high as I can up the platform rising above. But I don't spot him anywhere.

"Come on, Qhenno," I whisper.

This whole time, I've waited, imagining the worst things happening above.

I don't know what I expect. It's one man against an army. He's outnumbered. Yet...I hold on to hope that he can somehow pull through this.

My belly clenches, anxiety filling my gut as my pulse races.

The slaves rushing past all have a wildness in their eyes, as if fire has suddenly been breathed into them. I have never seen them so alive before. Not when we were given our rations. Not when any of them found the gems that would let them live another day.

"Hey!" I call out to one, trying to get his attention but he is busy rushing forward.

I hear a roar, a Morang somewhere above, and sounds of fighting. Grunts, screams of pain, before something big sways over the edge of the platform. A Morang. Many hands push him, too many to count, and his body goes akilter. My eyes widen as he topples, falling off the platform and into the abyss.

A roar goes through the mass of slaves heading higher on the platform—the guard's death like a drugged-up morale booster.

I grip the bars tighter, my pulse beating loudly in my ears as I press all my weight into the metal. It doesn't budge.

I can only hope the key wasn't on that guard that fell over.

As I draw back, bracing myself before I push against the bars again, something catches my gaze. Or, rather, *someone*.

The nymph-alien.

What is *she* doing here?

"Hey!" I shout. "Neturi!"

I have no clue if that's her name or her species, but her ears flick as she turns her panicked gaze from the crowd and finds me.

She hurries in my direction, immediately scanning the bars to find a way to get me out.

She pulls at them, but they don't budge.

"Have you seen my mate?" she asks, as she pulls on the bars again. "The Cambrian male you worked beside."

Eyes the color of lemon mixed with honey land on me and I shake my head slowly.

"Last I saw him, he was lower in the mine. Where the Morang sent us."

She jerks her chin once.

"What's happening?" I ask.

She blinks at me. "You don't know?"

When I shake my head, I see her gaze soften somewhat. "Your mate…he has started a coup. He killed the Morang leader…and we are fighting for our freedom."

Someone screams high above and I hear a Morang roar.

"He started a *what*…" My eyes widen. "Is he alright? Where is he?"

Her lips spread a little into a smile, her pointed ears folding to the sides of her head. "You have an honorable mate," she says. "You are lucky to have found such a male." Sobering, she glances behind her. "I am sorry. But I must seek my mate. I need to know he is alive. I will return once I have found him. To set you free."

I grip the bars, not wanting her to leave, but knowing I can't demand that she stay.

Nodding, I watch her climb away from the alcove and rush down the shaking platform.

Shit.

Will it even hold?

I watch her go, my heart rising in my throat.

Fuck.

I hope he's alright. Taking on those bastards by himself… He can't die now. Not when we're so close to getting out of here.

That's when I see him.

Standing at a curve in the platform, Qhenno faces in the opposite direction to where the crowd is heading. He faces me, and he stands there, looking at me.

Relief crashes into me like a runaway train.

My chest heaves, taking in a breath that's too big for my lungs.

"Qhenno!"

I don't know what this feeling is. It's a feeling that makes my entire body tingle, my heart beating an erratic rhythm that isn't sustainable.

And yet, it gives me life.

"Qhenno," I whisper as he begins pushing through the mob and toward me.

He has something in his hand. A weapon that looks like a mace that's far too large for any human to wield.

But he's not human.

He's Atari.

And he's a fucking god.

The moment he reaches me, he collapses to his knees.

I stretch my hands through the bars, reaching for him, this stranger who is making me feel all sorts of ways I can't seem to control.

He is covered in blood and I can't tell whether it is his or someone else's.

"Qhenno, you're bleeding." My voice shakes as I lift my hand and it's caked in red. "You're hurt."

For some reason, tears well in my eyes. I don't want him to die. And...I don't enjoy seeing him hurt, either.

He smiles at me, those black eyes twinkling.

"Your concern warms me, my ari," he says.

Reaching in, he cups my cheek and I tilt my head into his embrace.

"I need you to move backward, sweet thing. The last thing I want to do is hurt you."

I can only nod as he takes a step back, swinging the mace in his hand.

Even with the commotion happening in the background, I can only see him.

But this little prison is small. There's not much space I can put between me and the bars and when Qhenno sees this, I swear his visage becomes that of the grim reaper.

"Cover your head," he warns over the din, and I do as I'm told.

The first blow makes a deafening clang that makes my ears ring, and I jerk before wrapping my arms tighter over my head.

Another blow and there's a whine as metal bends.

Another blow, and pieces of metal fly in my direction, hitting me in the side.

Warm arms suddenly grip me and pull me against a hard chest, and I turn into him, holding him as tightly as he's holding me.

I don't protest as he shuffles backward, taking me with him.

Instead, I grip him tighter, because holding on to him is the only thing calming that erratic beat of my heart.

It's strange, it's new…but it doesn't feel wrong.

What's almost terrifying is how *right* it feels.

"You started a coup," I say, lifting my head as slaves rush past us, still heading higher up the platform, everyone taking arms.

"Anything for you," he replies.

I hold on to him as he drops the mace and continues walking downward.

I lift my head, great booming sounds going off above that echo straight down the mine shaft.

Was this it? Was this his plan all along?

I swallow hard, turning my gaze to him only to find he's focused on me. My heart swells, and my breath stops in my nose.

More slaves rush past us and the air grows colder.

He's walked ever farther down on the platform than I've ever been before.

"Aren't we going the wrong way?" I whisper.

Qhenno's lips shift slightly, a ghost of a smile passing over them as even more noise and booming sounds echo through the mine shaft.

"Forgive me, my ari," he says, his voice cutting through the commotion and into my senses.

"Wha—"

When he dips his head, his lips suddenly closing over mine, I don't know if I should squeal or melt. Instead, my entire body stiffens in shock, my eyes widening as I'm pulled flush against his chest. He moans into my mouth, his eyes rolling closed for a second before he grips my ass and presses me firmly against him.

Everything in the background becomes nothing as my world zones in on this one thing.

His lips.

His kiss.

It sends warmth right through me, igniting those feelings that were beginning to form like a match to gasoline.

Something thrums in my heart, like a pulse that isn't my own. It's such a strange feeling, but I don't get to think about it because we're suddenly tilting backward.

My eyes widen, a scream disappearing into Qhenno's mouth as he uses one hand to support the back of my head, forcing my lips to his.

He's kissing me…and it feels fucking phenomenal…but we've tilted backward so far that I'm facing the darkness of the abyss beyond.

He's losing his balance and we're going back too far! The platform's not broad enough! We're going to—

Gravity tilts.

"Qhenno!" I scream into his mouth

My heart leaves, expanding upward as we fall. Distantly, I hear someone scream, but I'm frozen in Qhenno's arms, my mouth still locked with his, my eyes wide as I see…*nothing*. We're falling, cold air rushing past us as we tumble into the abyss, the speed so strong that the air feels like shafts of ice itself.

We're falling…falling…*we're falling! We're going to die!*

The weightlessness, the speed of the fall, it's almost too much. Down we go, passing more of the platform that's so old it's broken into pieces, until there is nothing but pitch black.

Tears well into my eyes as I grip my only anchor. Him.

We turn in the air, or, at least, it feels like it. I can't see anything, but somehow, I can see *him*. I can *feel* him.

There is scorching heat under my palm, the back of his neck burning like a furnace, burning almost as brightly as his eyes.

Qhenno stares down at me and for a moment, I can see nothing else and nothing else matters.

We fall into the beyond, with nothing to hold on to but each other.

I expect the impact to be hard. For our skulls to crush the moment we hit the floor, but that's not what happens.

Instead, I see more of Qhenno's face. Like a rainbow strobe, his face is illuminated and I finally turn my blurry gaze to the space around us.

All along the walls, a light I've never seen before fills the space.

We're going so fast, it looks like a stream of fluorescent light.

I don't understand the light source until something flicks and lands on Qhenno's forehead. A…butterfly? With fins instead of wings?

My eyes widen some more. Lips still locked with Qhenno's, anything I try to say is smothered by his kiss.

The farther we fall, the more light I see. Thousands of little creatures appear, dotting the wall and emitting a colorful light from their wings.

For the first time since we fell, Qhenno releases his lips from mine.

"Hold your breath."

It's all the warning I get before we crash into ice-cold water.

Shock makes my body arch and I flail, reacting to the ice, to the cold, to the fact I am underwater and have no way to breathe. It's instinct, the way my chest jerks as I try to find the surface as we sink.

But I go nowhere. Qhenno is holding on to me, his legs propelling us through the cold with a speed that certainly isn't human.

The water, it's freezing and I already feel my body reacting. Seizing, going numb. The urge to breathe burns my lungs but I bury my head into Qhenno's chest and hope for the best.

I had no clue water was down here, but he obviously did.

This was his plan...

He pushes through the icy water as if he has fins and it's clear after a few moments that he's following the little water butterflies. I can see them now, lining the wall even under the water.

I almost don't feel it at first, but there is a current, a faint one, and hope is the only thing that stops my lungs from bursting. But when my body jerks, my chest burning with the need to breathe, some of that hope dies.

I need to breathe. I can't...I can't hold my breath for much longer.

I fight the urge, gripping on to Qhenno, with fingers so numb I can't feel them anymore. The only thing that makes me know I'm still alive is the constant burn, my chest caving in and cracking with the urge to inhale, and that warmth, that scorching warmth underneath my palm.

I focus on that warmth, I focus on him, until my body fails me, my instinct to pull in air overriding even my will.

Icy water rushes into my nose, my mouth, and fills my chest. I choke, but it only causes me to pull in more water. My eyes, my head, my chest, my lungs—everything burns.

I jerk against Qhenno, fighting to reach a surface that isn't there… and hoping…just hoping I can survive this.

But as I told him before…I don't believe in fate. It never works the way I want it to…

As that burn, that urge to breathe feels like it explodes in my head, I don't get to see us make it…

I want to live, but I don't get to see us breathe again…

14

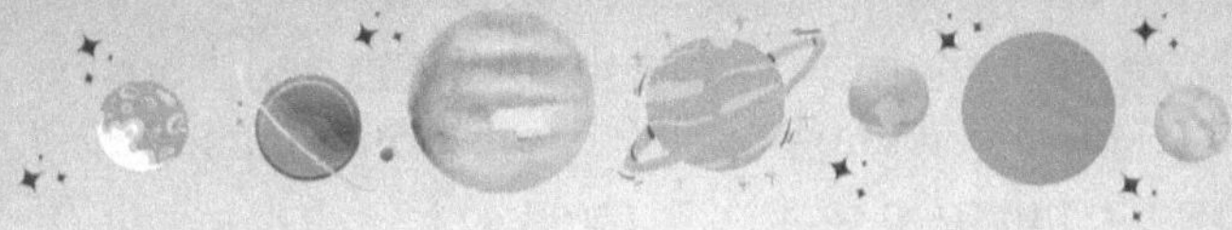

Qhenno

It takes far too long to reach the surface, and when I do, I almost forget to inhale. My life organ thumps hard in my chest with the effort it took to push through the icy torrent, but all I can focus on is the soft body I cradle to my chest.

Lifting Trudy higher against me, her body flops against mine and a pained ache shatters me from the inside out.

Supporting her head, I push toward the rocky shore before us, the current of the underground river taking me farther downstream than I would like.

Stay with me, my ari.

In this large cavern, little *flendrils* line the rocks, bathing the area in their bioluminescent light.

It's because of their light that I can see my female's face has gone slack…see how deathly pale her skin has turned…and see the very image of death creeping over her.

Don't leave me.

Splashing toward the shore, panic shoots through my frame and I almost stumble with her in my arms.

I manage to stay on my feet, my life organ thumping for a thousand beings as I stagger onto the shore and set her down.

Ice-cold water runs off me as I look at her, my chest heaving. I can still feel her life force. It is stronger now, my sense of it, and I tug on that invisible cord that is growing to bind us together.

There, thrumming along its length, is the very faint beat of her pulse. I hold on to it at the very same time that I place my palm at the center of her chest.

"Come my, ari," I whisper. "Come back to me."

Her life organ thumps underneath my palm and I hold on to that bond deep inside me before pressing down firmly on her chest, forcing her life organ to pump in tune with mine.

Once, twice, I do the same thing, but nothing happens.

Again. I must try again.

That sliver of fear settling at the base of my spine won't take root. I refuse to consider that…that I'm *losing* her.

My chest heaves, breaths coming harder than my lungs can afford, and I feel for my mate's pulse once more and give it a push through the bond that we have.

Nothing happens.

Desolation seeps into my soul.

I do the only other thing I can think of. Tipping my head to hers, I capture her lips in mine once more.

Unlike before, when they were supple and warm, now they are stiff and cold. Unyielding, they resist as I push my breath down her throat.

Come on, my ari.

My life organ feels like hard rock in my chest. The lifeblood in my veins turns to ice as I pause and press down on her chest, once, twice, three more times.

Manual resuscitation.

I have never had to use this method to revive anyone. It is archaic, and I wonder if it will work now, but I have no other tools with me. The communicator in my trou has no defibrillator.

This has to work.

Placing my lips over hers once more, I breathe deep and give her my air.

When I ease up to pump her chest, Trudy suddenly coughs.

My whole body shakes as she heaves beneath me.

"Trudy," I groan.

She coughs and turns, her body expelling water as she tries to pull in breaths. Her eyes are red and watery as she inhales deeply, her gaze finding mine.

"Trudy," I say again.

Grasping the back of her neck, I support her head as her body adjusts to breathing once more. Her chest continues to heave as she shivers, her eyes scrunching closed as she coughs.

Pulling her against me, I give her all the warmth my body can provide and she grips my chest, those small fingers of hers digging into me.

"I took a great risk," I mutter, holding her close.

Even though she's breathing again, it hasn't calmed the storm that's begun roiling in my chest. Maybe I should have stayed in that mine shaft...gone upwards with the mob and fought the reinforcements that were arriving. But even with the slaves at my back, I couldn't risk the Morang taking Trudy away from me. Not again.

"My ari...you must be livid."

I never considered it before I jumped off that platform, but the thought comes to me now. If she was so keen to reject me before, she's surely going to do it now. But that thought is of little consequence. I can live with her rejection, even if it tears me apart.

She is alive, and that's all that matters.

Pulling in a deep breath, Trudy coughs some more.

"A-are you alright?" she asks before more coughing overtakes her.

She's asking about me. In her state, she's wondering about *my* well-being.

After another deep inhale and more coughing, I cradle her head, a purr developing deep in my chest. It's all I can do to comfort her. After all, I'm the reason she is in distress.

It takes a few moments before her body calms enough for her gaze to dart around the cave.

"Where are we?"

"Somewhere underground, far from the mine."

Her gaze flicks back to me, eyes going wide. "What?"

I grip her closer, the fact I almost lost her still fresh in my mind. "I saw the scans of this city before I arrived. I knew this river runs below it."

There's silence as Trudy shudders against me and then…

"You did it," she whispers. "You got us out of there."

She doesn't mention that it was at great risk and I don't know whether to be thankful or to own up to the danger I put her through.

When her shivering hand reaches up to cradle my cheek, I almost groan at the pleasure of the contact.

"Thank you," she whispers, her eyes glowing with fresh water that's not because of the strain she's just endured.

She throws both arms around my shoulders, pulling me in, and I welcome it, burying my face into the crook of her neck.

"Thank you so much!"

A groan rumbles through me as I nuzzle her skin.

But my mate is cold. She's shivering. I can't take this moment to enjoy even these little touches.

I must get her warmth immediately.

Taking one last nuzzle, I inhale her skin before lifting my head to look around the cavern.

The *flendrils'* light creates a comforting glow that makes it easy to see, and as Trudy's body calms, I sense when her head tilts and she starts looking around too.

I see the spot we need to move to seconds later. It's away from the river's shore, farther into the cave, but in a nook that will be easier to defend should any nuisances come our way.

Easing up, I grasp Trudy to me and stand.

She makes a soft little sound and digs her icy fingers into my torso.

I don't complain. I want her touches. All of them. Painful or filled with pleasure. I want it all.

But she's so qeffing cold…I know we're not out of danger yet. Her health is my priority and worry begins crawling into my mind as I head toward the nook I spotted.

My mate is supposed to be in our lodging, surrounded by soft things and warmth. Not in a cold cavern, shivering, near death.

My life organ aches as I set her down. Thankfully, the earth here is dry.

When I glance at her, those strange eyes of hers are watching me with…awe and expectation.

"We should keep going," she says.

I shake my head. "Not like this. Your health is waning. I can feel it."

She swallows hard. "What if the Morang find us here?"

I huff a small laugh through my nose. "If any of them survive the mob, I doubt they will willingly jump into this river. It is safer for them to go around."

She dips her chin to her chest in acceptance, but I can tell she is unsure.

But she has no need to worry. I will keep her safe.

Moving toward the spot I saw, I set her down.

Leaving her there is hard, even though I am moving only a few arm lengths away.

That skin at the back of my neck aches and pulses, feeling like a scorching rod at the top of my spine. Soon, it will become unbearable, the need to mark my mate driving me to the point of insanity.

But she is a female I am willing to accept insanity for.

Glancing back at Trudy while I search for any rocks and kindling I can find, her soft face as she watches me makes me yearn to return to her side. She wraps her arms around herself and does not complain.

I want to get to know her better. I want her to get to know *me*.

I want her to *want* me…because I have been waiting for her all my life…and…in the few moments in her presence…I already want her more than anything else.

Arms filled with enough materials from plants long gone, I head back to my mate's side. Her gaze falls to the items in my arms and she nods.

"A fire?" she asks.

"Yes, my ari."

"I can help," she states, and to my horror, she begins to shuffle my way, her body jerking and shivering still.

"No!"

She freezes and guilt immediately fills me at the tone of my voice.

Closing my eyes for a moment, I calm myself. "You must stay there. I don't want you to—"

"To get in your way."

When my gaze flicks to her, there's an expression on her face that I've seen only on Bhihan's face whenever he thinks no one is looking. Pain. Pain that is hidden.

Dropping the items in my arms, I move closer to her, and my life organ cracks as she flinches away from me.

"It's okay," she says, "I understand."

No, she doesn't.

Crouching before her, I take one of her trembling hands in mine, but her gaze remains averted.

"You were slack in my arms..." I state. "I *saw* your life force leaving."

She looks at me then, her gaze unreadable.

"You're mine to protect. Mine to keep safe. Please...I cannot do much in these circumstances...but...let me take care of you."

Her lips part, a slight tremble on them, as she gives me a hesitant nod.

I offer her the best expression of assurance that I can as I turn and begin to arrange the rocks and kindling.

Luckily, I still have my communicator hidden in the depths of my trou. I'll be able to use it to make a spark and after that, to find a path from this cavern and to the surface where I'll head toward our ship.

Trudy watches me as I finish arranging the kindling and fish my communicator from my trou. The spark is easy to make and soon there's a crackle.

I nurse it, adding more kindling as I hear Trudy shuffle closer to the warmth.

"Pretty handy gadget," she whispers.

I glance over my shoulder to find she's shuffled close enough that she's almost touching me.

"I've had it since the first war."

I can feel her gaze on me. "How many wars have you fought in?"

I grunt, a soft smile coming to my lips. "Too many to count. Atar wasn't always the great world it is now."

"And you fought here too…for *me*… As Neturi said, you are an honorable male."

My life organ pulses, my fangs aching as my gaze slips to her.

"That is not a word I would use to describe myself. I am only a male that fights for what is dear to me."

And *she* is dear to me. She doesn't know it yet, but she's mine. And I would do anything for her.

Her pale skin grows rosy at the cheeks, another slight tremor going through her lips before she pulls them into her mouth.

"Come, sit near the fire." I turn and rise, moving out of the way.

"What about you?"

"You are my priority, my ari."

She shivers at my words but nods and moves closer to the fire. Stretching her hands toward it, she rubs them together and releases a breath through her mouth before flashing me a smile.

My life organ blooms.

She is not angry with me? Turned off even? For all I have done?

Controlling my fury was so difficult, I displayed it to her more than once in that mine. She has seen the ruthless male I can be…yet…she is smiling at me.

There is hope yet.

But despite that, I will work hard to show her I can be a suitable mate. I will work hard to show her I am worthy of more of her smiles.

15

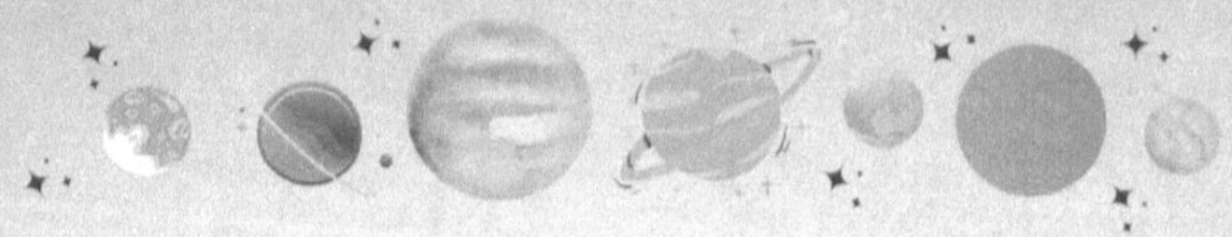

Trudy

This big alien is confusing.

He moves around the cave, gathering things that have washed up along the shore, bits of wood and other brambles, and brings them back to the fire, feeding it until it is crackling and bright.

He doesn't stop. Every time I think he will rest, he is moving again, searching for other things. Before I know it, he's found enough driftwood to make a good pile that will last a few hours.

Shuffling closer to the fire, I try to warm myself as much as I can. But my clothes are still wet and even though I've been sitting here for a while, that's hardly changed.

I need to take my clothes off…

Eyeing Qhenno, I wonder if I should.

All that's happened between us…it's so confusing.

Growling at myself, I roll my eyes.

He's fought hard for me more times in the short days I've known him than my own people on Earth ever have. Who cares about being modest?

When a particularly strong shiver makes my teeth clatter, I push my inhibitions away.

Eyeing a section of rock jutting from the earth close to where I sit, I decide. I can spread the clothes over it and the warmth should still be able to reach them.

One more glance in Qhenno's direction and I note his back is turned to me while he digs for something. He's been digging for a while.

Shuffling out of my blouse is easy and when I slip it off, leaving only my bra underneath, I hold it up to the light.

It's torn in many places, the lower end shredded from where I'd ripped it in several places to make the bindings for my hands.

Sighing, I pull myself closer to the rock and drape the blouse over it.

Next are my trousers. Those are harder because I have to maneuver my legs, but with enough twisting and grunting, I pull them off.

A shiver goes through me, causing me to tremble now that I'm only in underwear, but I drape the trousers over the rock too and drag myself closer to the fire.

I sit dangerously close to it as I wrap my arms around myself, and soon, my body begins to warm.

Releasing a breath, I tilt my head back and gaze up at the cave roof.

If I'd known this river was here all along, would I have had the courage to jump?

The little water butterflies have lit the entire space, making the roof look like a kaleidoscope. I've never seen anything like it before...nor anything like the little creatures themselves.

It's...beautiful, and I find myself staring it at for far too long, almost forgetting that I'm not alone.

Eyes darting over to where Qhenno was digging, my throat goes dry when I find his eyes on me.

Another shiver goes through me, and this time, it's not because I'm cold.

Even from where he kneels, I can see the heat growing in his gaze as he stares at me. That same look he'd had when he was in the mine. As if he wants to possess me, his mouth watering just staring at me...

I swallow hard, remembering the shock of his lips pressed against mine… How he kissed me hard before he jumped over that platform.

Something flutters in my belly and I almost wonder if I swallowed one of the water butterflies.

I try not to stare at him as he rises slowly, something in his hand. But I can't even focus on what he's found, because I can't take my gaze away from his.

It's the light, right? And the distance? Because I swear his eyes have gone black again, like a demon's. The only other times I've seen him do that, he'd killed someone right before, or right after.

As he begins heading in my direction, that shiver goes down through me once more.

He stops walking toward me, his throat moving, and even though I can't see his pupils, I get the sense that his gaze is moving down my body ever so slowly. I can feel it travel over my skin, sending tingling sensations through me like a wave that's come to shore.

"Qhenno?" I whisper.

Should I be afraid right now? I wasn't mistaken…his eyes *have* gone black and I don't think it's a result of the cold.

Am I in danger? But even as that question flies through my mind, I know I'm the safest I've ever been.

I don't feel fear…I feel…*anticipation*.

Right now, the male before me looks nothing like the kind male who's been sticking his neck out for me and endangering his life to get me out of hell.

This male in front of me looks…*possessed*.

His mouth opens in a low growl that should make me pack my shit up and get the hell out of here. Instead, it holds me transfixed.

I watch as his fangs descend, dripping clear fluid that he swipes away with his tongue, a rumble going through him.

I don't know why, but my gaze finally moves to slide down his frame. The muscles bunched in his torso, his fists holding some kind of shelled creature, and the way he's standing as if he'll pounce if I even move an inch.

Some instinct inside tells me to keep still, as if I am a mouse hiding from a cat. And I do. I don't move. I don't even breathe.

"Qh-Qhenno?" I call his name again, some fear leaking into my voice, and that's when his gaze flicks back to gold. The movement is so sudden, it's almost as if I imagined those pitch-black pits. "Are you ok?"

His gaze falls to my heaving chest, to my breasts almost spilling out of my bra, and his throat moves.

"I have found sustenance," he finally says, his limbs becoming more fluid as he walks toward me.

His throat moves again as he pulls his gaze away from me, keeping his eyes pointed at the ground as he approaches.

My brow furrows slightly.

"Humans don't have mates."
"But Atari do…"

Those words repeat in my head for the third time and I can't move as Qhenno comes to sit across from me.

The fire's light plays across his face and chest as he sets down two shelled creatures. Smooth and oval, the shells have a hole at the top, but there's no indication as to what's inside them.

Qhenno's gaze slides to me only briefly as his throat moves once more and he looks away, a shudder going through him.

"Sorry about your tunic," I whisper, not knowing what to say and maybe too afraid to ask the important question. "I left it in the alcove back in the mine."

Qhenno shrugs. "I have many more on the ship."

"Ship?"

"The mother ship. The Zarzenius." He glances at me once more, his gaze slipping to my lips before he focuses on the shelled creatures before him. "You will see it soon. Once we leave this place."

I can't even imagine…

There's a crack that makes me jerk as Qhenno drives the shelled creature into the rock beside us. The shell partly shatters and he makes a low sound in his chest, one that makes something tingle between my legs.

I clear my throat as he then places the shell into the fire, the cracked side up.

He does the same to the other shell before easing back and resting his hands on his knees, his gaze sliding to me as if he can't force himself to look away any longer.

For a moment, we stare at each other, neither saying a word, and warmth rushes to my cheeks.

We don't have the disturbances of that mine between us any longer. Now it's just him and me in this small, silent little cave.

Pulling my gaze from his, I adjust my aching body, wincing a little as I turn one of my legs.

A warm hand closes around my wrist and I jerk in surprise. He moved so fast—

"Do they ache?" he asks. Close, too close. I can smell that fresh scent of his and it is one I haven't forgotten.

"D-do what ache?"

His fingers release me and brush over one of my legs, sending a lump into my throat immediately.

"Your legs."

There's no judgment in his voice, only curiosity. Forcing the lump down, I try to answer him, pushing the defensiveness that usually rises with mention of my legs away.

"They get cold sometimes. The…the uh…circulation is bad in them."

Qhenno makes another sound in his throat, his gaze flicking to me for a second.

His fingers skate over my thigh and I shudder at the ghost of feeling that echoes from his touch.

"You can feel," he says. "Sensation is not lost."

I shake my head, licking my lips. "Uh, yea…I can feel…a little. But I can't lift them…or stand…or walk. They're too weak."

He makes that sound in his throat again that makes my belly twist.

"I will soothe them for you."

My eyes bug out as he suddenly moves to kneel over me, my legs between his thighs.

"What are you—"

Warm hands grip my thighs and knead slowly, sending warmth through my leg.

"Qhenno, you…you don't have to—"

"I *want* to." There's a growl in his lips, one that doesn't sound hostile even though it should, and when his gaze flashes to me, his eyes have gone pitch black again.

I stare at him, my own eyes widening as I watch him massage my legs.

"Your eyes…"

His throat moves and his hands pause on my leg before they continue moving again.

"Do not fear…I will not mark you against your will."

Mark me?

That uneasy feeling that keeps twisting my gut comes back in full force as I watch him lift my leg so he can knead and massage my calf. Another lump forms in my throat and the words leave my lips before I can stop them.

"Is it because…you think I'm your mate?"

When his hands freeze and he doesn't answer, I know I've hit the nail on the head. *I'm right. This explains everything.*

Something deep inside me curdles and spasms, a pain that has no real source spreading through my frame.

"Is that why you've searched for me so long? Put yourself in so much danger?"

He doesn't respond. God knows, he doesn't even move.

"You think I'm someone special to you…" I whisper, the horror of that reality hitting me with full force, because in this short time… maybe he's become someone special to me too.

"You are wrong," he finally says, those dark eyes enveloping me. "I didn't know you were mine until I held you in my arms."

"But…"

"But you do not want a mate," he states, his gaze falling as he continues to massage me, moving to the other leg. "I am aware."

I swallow hard, not missing the note of pain and sorrow in his voice.

We fall into silence, only the sound of the river rushing by and the soft crackling of the fire make a backdrop that whispers in the cave.

I bite my tongue several times, multiple things I could say coming to my mind, but none of them seem appropriate. Instead, I watch him work.

The more his fingers move over my skin, the more I tingle inside.

"Even with my limb difference...you still think I'm your mate?" I finally ask.

I don't know how it works. The concept is fairly new to us New Earth inhabitants. The thought of a mate that's perfect for you... someone whose soul was made to travel with yours...has always had me wondering.

To have someone declaring I'm theirs because destiny intended it... is hard to believe.

For a few moments, I don't realize Qhenno has stopped moving, his eyes on me. They've gone back to their golden color but are completely unreadable.

"What limb differences?" he asks.

I point at my legs. "Do I really have to say it?"

That unreadable look in his eyes doesn't change as he gazes at me long enough that I want to squirm.

"Why would your differences matter?" he finally says.

My tongue must be stuck in my throat because I have no response. I blink at him, trying to find an answer, but there is none.

His words split my world and break me apart, revealing my most vulnerable areas. Those spots I've hidden and protected, and anxiety rises within me at this sudden openness.

But he's right, why should my differences matter? He's Atari. I am human. He has fangs. I do not. He has claws. I do not. He's tall and strong while I am small and weak in comparison.

All my life, my differences to other humans has defined my existence. And suddenly, this male...he is here asking me a question I have always asked myself.

Why should my difference matter?

There's a sizzle and a pop that breaks the tension between us and I glance over almost with relief to see the clam, or whatever it is, bubbling and frothing.

Qhenno sets my leg down and reaches for my damp blouse.

"I hope you don't mind," he says. When I shake my head, he dips his hand into the fire as if the flames don't exist, and pulls out the steaming shell.

Pulling out the other, he sets it on the rock before wrapping my blouse around the first. Blowing on it lightly, he brings it toward my lips.

"Take your time," he says. "I do not want you to burn those precious lips."

16

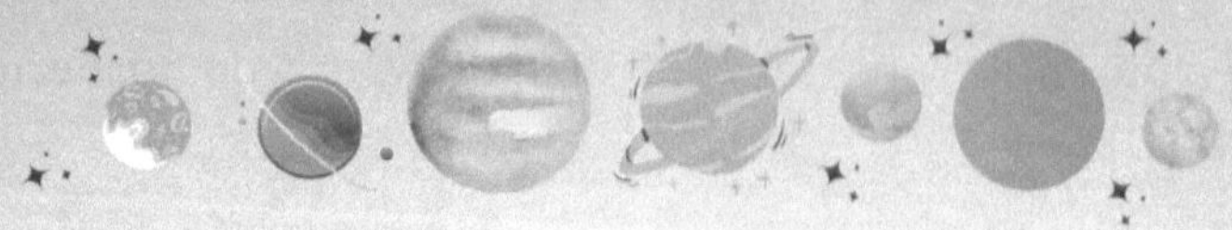

Qhenno

Her tongue is so small and pink.

With tentative little flicks, she takes the *sand goosh* into her mouth with tiny sips.

I am happy she is eating it. I wish I could give her better, but the *goosh* will at least give her some energy before we have to leave this place.

While scouting for kindling and food, I searched the recesses of this small cave. There is only one narrow shaft that possibly leads above ground—too small for either of us to fit in, even if we take the risk.

And I am not ready to risk her life again.

As Trudy eats, she releases a soft sound in her throat, one that makes my hand tighten on the goosh's shell.

"Mm, what is this? It's good."

"Goosh." I have to clear my throat lest I sound like a creature from the depths that's come to steal her soul.

She makes that sound again and before I can hold it back, a whimper leaves my throat.

Qef. I hope she didn't hear that. The last thing I want is for her to feel unsafe around me.

I couldn't hide it. She knows she is my mate now...and she must know the thoughts going through my head.

She's shed her clothing and her soft skin is beckoning me to touch her. It is so thin...I want to run my tongue over her if only to see her turn pink underneath the warmth of it.

But I can control myself. This urge.

"Aren't you going to have any?" Those striking eyes of hers rise to meet mine. So soft, they make a wave of warmth flood through me.

"Later," I growl.

Her throat moves and a beat passes before she closes her lips around the fleshy bit of the goosh and sucks the warm juices out.

I hold a breath.

It doesn't help that the tip of the goosh is flared like the head of my cock. Now, all I can see is her mouth closing over my tip. Another growl rumbles through me and I fight to keep my gaze averted from her.

But if she's scared, she isn't showing it.

When not even half of the goosh is finished, she pushes at my hand lightly.

"Thank you," she whispers.

I stare at the goosh. There is so much left.

"You do not have to deny yourself for me," I say to her. "I have prepared the other for myself...and if you want that one too, you can have it. I am sure I can find more if I look hard enough."

Her cheeks heat and her lips twist into a smile that makes another wave of warmth wash over me.

"No...you don't understand. I'm full. Maybe another day, I could eat more, but I think after everything, I am too tired." She plasters her palm on her belly and rubs it.

I can almost feel the need bleed into my gaze just staring at that spot. So soft, her palm presses into her flesh, and then she...shudders.

Qef me. I have been so focused on feeding her, I haven't been stoking the fire. Setting the goosh down, I push more driftwood into the flames. But when I turn to look at my mate, she is still shuddering, albeit, trying to hide it.

"You are cold," I whisper.

She grants me one more of her smiles and I soak in it like a *mefekki* hoarding Arzentus. "Only just a little. It can't be helped."

The piece of driftwood in my hand falls into the fire as suddenly as I release it. Trudy's eyes widen as I rise, hook my fingers into the waist of my trou, and pull it down.

Her mouth falls open, her eyes widening even more on my nakedness, but there is still no fear in her gaze.

Good. That will make this easier.

"What are you doing?" Her whisper is so low, it's almost as if she hasn't asked a question. But her eyes are glued to my shaft. Erect and pointed forward, I pause.

I didn't consider that part before I took off my trou.

I am different from her Earthkin males. Of that I am sure. It is the one part of my anatomy that might shock her. My flared head…the ridges that run along the shaft…

And…maybe the size.

I hope I am bigger than others she has seen…and I hope that pleases her.

She stares at it and a throb goes along the length, making it jerk so hard it slaps into my belly, a string of preseed making a bridge between my torso and the tip.

"I—" she begins, the uncertainty finally finding its way into her voice.

"Do not worry," I say. "I promise you, my ari, I will not do anything you don't want me to."

She blinks, warmth filling her cheeks. "Well…what are you going to do right now?"

I release a soft grunt. "Make myself useful."

As I move to lie beside her, Trudy's eyes grow even larger. Large enough for some humor to twist my lips.

When I reach for her, pulling her body on top of mine, she lets out a soft surprised sound.

"This is…"

"Uncomfortable?" I ask. Settling her on top of me, the moment her body touches mine, I have to stifle a groan. "We have done this before."

Seeing her softness is one thing. Feeling her pressed against me like this is another.

Shifting her legs so her entire frame is on my own, I try to remain focused.

Qef, this is harder to do than I expected.

"No...not that." If anything, her cheeks have grown even warmer. "You weren't naked that time..."

I don't know what that means, but I hope it means she is warming up to me.

I wrap my arms around her, pulling her into my warmth and, to my surprise, she rests her head on my chest and inhales deeply.

"Do all Atari act like this with their mates?" she says after a few moments.

I grunt. "I hope not."

She lifts her head then, those eyes of hers searching mine. "What do you mean?"

"A mate is supposed to be kept warm and safe, not—"

Not wet and cold in a cave with no food or safety...

Trudy rests her head. "I'm not complaining," she says, her icy fingers moving up to my chest, tracing a pattern I can't determine and I hold my breath once more.

"Your eyes have gone black again..." she whispers.

I resist the urge to groan as the movement of her fingers becomes almost painfully pleasurable.

"Does it not make you afraid of me?"

She hesitates and I brace myself for the impact of her words.

"I have...never been scared of you."

I freeze.

"Not once..." She pauses. "Well, actually once. When I spilled the drinks on your shoes."

A breath of relief shudders from me.

"And now...?" It's a question I shouldn't ask. One that will only shatter me if her answer isn't favorable.

Trudy tilts her head up, her eyes finding mine. Need threatens to overcome me. I know all she's looking into are the black lust-filled eyes of a mate she doesn't want.

"You're so sure I'm your mate…" she whispers.

My life organ stutters as if waiting for her to continue. She hasn't answered my question. I know not whether this is good or bad.

"How are you so sure?" That small hand of hers moves up to my jaw, tracing the angle of it right down to my chin. Her eyes narrow somewhat, her gaze drifting off to a faraway place even though she is looking right at me. "How do you know when you've found your mate? And how can *I* be your mate…I'm not even Atari."

I grip that hand that's at my chin probably too suddenly, because she jerks against me, her gaze zoning back into the present.

Bringing her hand down to where my life organ beats, I press her palm against my skin.

"With Atari…we know the moment we first meet our mates. It's…a sensation like no other. As if a cord that's been spun has gripped your life organ and you cannot be without her." Trudy shudders against me and I draw her closer to me with my free hand. "You are human…you cannot feel the bond…not yet…not until…"

"Not until what?" Voice so soft, it whispers over my skin, pushing my control.

"Until I mark you."

I expect her to pull away. To push me away from her and scold me for mentioning the mark yet again. For a mate like me, one she does not want, I shouldn't be mentioning such a thing.

A mark binds…whether or not the mate consents. Once I mark her, she is mine. Forever.

Whether she wants me or not.

But Trudy does the most surprising thing.

With her other hand, she reaches up, her palm resting against the sensitive skin at the back of my neck.

"Trudy," I groan, ready to warn her that touching me there is a bad idea. It will not only spur my arousal, it will make me even hungrier for her. I will become insatiable. It is my weakest spot.

But the words don't leave my mouth. No other words leave my mouth as her soft lips brush against mine.

Now, I don't even *dare* to breathe.

I have tried not to focus on the memory of her lips against mine. Locked those thoughts away, for they will drive me crazy. But now, here she is, blessing me with the press of those soft bits of flesh against mine once more.

She's no longer in the frigid water and in need of my breath.

She is doing this…because she *wants* to?

When that little pink tongue of hers flicks into my mouth, I can resist no longer. A groan erupts from my chest as I grip the back of her head with one hand and meet her tongue with my own.

A soft moan leaves her frame and she shudders as I grip her plump ass with my other hand. The feel of her softness under my palm makes my length throb, and another groan escapes my lips.

"So perfect," I whisper delving my tongue into her mouth. Trudy moans, taking the invasion with a little whimper before she pushes against my chest, forcing me to release her.

Soft pants heave both our chests as she stares down at me and I wonder if I went too far.

"Do you mean that?" she pants.

I stare at her. At her beauty. She is even more than I dreamed of. I'm a lucky qeffer to have found her on time. For her to be *mine*.

"Qhenno," her voice implores. "Did you mean what you just said."

I blink, the need coursing through me abating for a few seconds.

I have no memory of what I just said…

"About me being perfect…" Trudy whispers.

My life organ thumps so hard in my chest, I swear she feels it.

"Yes," I croak, the emotions almost overwhelming. "I will prove myself worthy of your matehood. I will—"

My words are cut off as her lips close over mine again. And this time, it isn't like her first tentative kiss.

Trudy nibbles on my lips, making my eyes roll over, making my need rumble through the cave, echoing against the walls, disturbing the flendrils that rest there so their fins shake, making a wave of colors cascade over us.

Her tongue dives into my mouth once more and when I return her kiss, she releases a soft moan, her hands finding themselves in the strands of my hair.

"Trudy…"

We must slow down.

My eyes roll back again, the sensation of her soft body on mine almost sending me into insanity.

"Trudy…"

I grip her tighter.

I will not be able to control myself. I must cease.

"Show me." Trudy's words cut through my consciousness like a snizz's whip.

Surely, I did not hear right.

"Show me, Qhenno," she whispers again. "Show me what it feels like to be loved by a male like you."

17

Trudy

I must've gone crazy too…Qhenno's insanity spreading to me…

But the feeling that's overcoming me is one I have felt many times before, only, not like this.

This male who I've only just met has opened the door to the vulnerabilities I've hidden for so long. In this short time, he's made me *feel*.

And I…I can't deny that despite that I know this might not be real…that I *want* it to be real.

I fucking want it and it's breaking me apart.

"Show me, Qhenno… Show me what it feels like to be loved by a male like you…"

At my words, Qhenno freezes beneath me and I swallow hard. Have I gone too far? Did I read his signals wrong?

But I can feel *it* at the apex of my thighs. Feel it throbbing. Feel how hot and velvety and *hard* he is.

He wants this…doesn't he?

I get my answer shortly after when a rumble goes through his entire frame, one that makes me vibrate on his chest like I'm sitting on top of one of those machines the people of Old Earth used for their laundry.

I gasp, gripping on to him as he suddenly grabs my thighs and pulls me higher against his torso.

Now head-to-head, those dark eyes of his should look evil and otherworldly. Instead, they send a shiver through me that ends up right at the center of my thighs, finding that little bud nestled between my folds and making it swell and throb.

"Qhenno..." I breathe.

He growls, tilting his head into my neck and inhaling deeply.

The hot slickness of his tongue as it flicks out over my sensitive skin has me gasping, my back arching as he holds me to him.

"Trudy...my mate...you know not what you request."

I gulp. His voice...it's gone so deep. It sends another shiver right through me.

"You ask for something you are not ready for..." he continues, his gaze flicking from black to gold, then black again.

Oh...but I *am* ready. I'm half-naked in a cave on top of the sexiest male I've ever seen in my life, and I'm not even scared.

How readier can I be?

"Please," I whimper.

I don't know when I moved from almost literally drowning to now drowning in need, but my whole body feels like it's being powered by some form of energy outside of myself.

It rides my skin in waves. Every piece of me that is touching this male feels like it's on fire and the only way to put it out is to let him touch me more.

"Qhenno," I breathe, "I *want* this."

He makes another low sound in his throat before that hand that's grasping my ass gives me a squeeze.

I whimper.

I'm not a small female, but he has me on top of him as if I'm a precious little thing. The way he holds me there, his body shuddering underneath mine only creates electricity in the air that I can feel move over my skin.

When his fingers slip underneath my panties, moving over my skin in a way that makes my breaths stutter, hot thick need swells in my center like it's been called from deep within me.

"Trudy," he groans into my neck. He licks the same spot again before closing his mouth over it and sucking on my flesh.

At the same time, his hand slips down through my panties to palm me whole.

"Qef me," he mutters into my neck. "You're even softer here."

One finger swirls through my folds, making me whimper, my eyes closing as I feel him explore my most vulnerable spot.

"And slick," he murmurs. When my eyes open, those dark eyes of his lock with mine. A delicious rumble goes through his chest. "Is this slick for me?"

My cheeks warm, a whimper of pleasure going through me when he slowly slides one of his digits inside me. "Oh gods...qef me..." he murmurs, not taking his eyes off mine. "So slick and tight."

I feel like a plant that's blooming. Something shivers through me, going through my entire frame to culminate right where his fingers are, and I clench on his digit.

Qhenno freezes. It's like he doesn't even breathe as he stares at me.

"What did you just do?" his voice is so thick with need, it is hoarse and deep. More like a growl than anything else.

I do it again. I clench on his finger, my eyes rolling back for a moment at the feel of it deep inside me.

Slowly, his lip curls slightly, his fangs descending as I watch.

"You should get off me now," he says, even as his finger begins to stroke through my slickness. "You should roll off and let me leave this place," he pants. "I will go into the cold water. I will stay there until I can control myself once more."

But even as he speaks, his eyes grow impossibly darker when he slides a second finger into me and I whimper at the shot of pleasure it sends through my bones.

"Trudy..." he groans. "Go."

As if I can move—and this has nothing to do with my legs.

"I don't want to," I manage to say.

Qhenno growls, pushing his fingers into me right down to the knuckle.

My back arches, a cry leaving my lips when his thumb finds my clit.

"So tight. So wet. Is this all for me, my mate?"

I nod, words failing me.

"Do you want this?" His eyes flick back to gold and I grip his jaw with both hands, my chest heaving as I look down into his face.

"Yes," I whisper.

Qhenno gulps and I can see the doubt entering his gaze.

But it's the truth.

I want what he's offering. I feel I might die without it.

Dipping my head, I fuse my lips with his, accepting the rumble that he releases into my mouth. He grips me tighter, his fingers moving deep within me as he fucks me slowly with those two digits, his thumb making slow circles against my clit.

I whimper when he increases the pace, pulling my lips from his as a cry leaves my throat.

"Gods…you're beautiful…" Qhenno groans.

The orgasm that crashes through me comes from nowhere and everywhere at once. My eyelids flutter as I collapse against him, and though it's given me some clarity, I know it's not enough. I want more.

Reaching between us, I grasp the tip of that rod that's been burning like a furnace against me.

Qhenno jerks in my touch, his eyes widening and flicking from gold to black.

As I push my panties away and position him at my entrance, I stare into his eyes.

There are so many emotions there, communicated even underneath the darkness that's overtaken his pupils.

Pain. Need. Want. And hope. So much hope.

As his fingers slip from within me and I line up the flared tip of his cock with my entrance, I pause. Doubt entering my mind for the first time.

"You're so small," he says, his voice strange and strained.

"Yes," I whisper…and that's exactly why I've hesitated. I didn't think about it before, but the tip of his cock is flared. It covers my entire pussy. How the hell will I get it in?

He must sense my unsurety because his hand suddenly closes around mine.

There's something intimate about the way he guides himself in my hand, positioning that flared head at that—

"Tight little hole," he growls, speaking my thoughts. "Relax, my mate. I will not hurt you."

As he pushes between my fingers, his tip slides against the center of my palm, fucking my hand.

My pussy quivers, sensing the nearness of it, and just the sensation of him moving against my palm already has my throat going dry.

"Now," he whispers as he pushes through my fist, the flared tip of his cock lining up with my entrance.

I brace for the intrusion as he slowly pushes into me.

The flared head bends and folds as he pulls back and pushes in a little more, molding itself to me. It feels like a gigantic fist that's forcing itself inside me and my mouth opens as I stop breathing and can only feel.

"Come here my sweetness," Qhenno murmurs, pulling me back down to him.

His lips capture mine as he pulls his hips back and pushes further in.

Ridges that run along the length of him make my eyes roll back as his hips begin to find a rhythm.

Finally releasing his length, I lift my hands to his head, my fingers resting on that soft warm spot at the back of his neck. As soon as I make contact with that spot, his hips jerk, thrusting him all the way inside me.

A cry leaves my lips, pleasure being mixed in with pain and I can only thank the gods that he doesn't move further. He freezes, his jaw clenches, and he grips me tighter.

"Have I...have I hurt you, my ari?"

Sweet honey feels like it's building in my cunt. "No, Qhenno. Please...don't stop."

There is only a moment where my words seem to register before his thrusts begin deep and slow until I'm rocking back and forth on top of him.

Slick surrounds my entrance, the friction pushing it between my folds and over that tight little bud that grinds against his pubic bone with every thrust he makes.

My eyes roll back in my head, pleasure I didn't know existed crashing through my frame.

When he pulls me closer to him, closing his mouth over my neck, his fangs brush over my skin. The feel of them sends another deep moan through me.

He could bite me right now. Draw blood.

The thought of it, and the way he gently licks and sucks on the spot makes my pussy quiver. Gripping my ass with both hands, Qhenno forces me down on him. Sweet honey erupts in my slit and another peak rises and crashes through me.

"Qhenno!" I scream his name at the same time that he...*roars.*

He pistons hard into me before slamming his hips upward, forcing us even tighter together as his cock spasms so hard, I know jets of cum are releasing inside me.

His roar echoes throughout the cave, sending the water butterflies into a frenzy as they fly off the cave roof to swirl all around us.

It's such a beautiful scene. Everything about it is...*beautiful.*

I can't stop the barrage of emotions before they hit me. Can't help the sob that suddenly racks through me the moment Qhenno shudders and lowers his hips back to the ground.

Tears run down my cheek, falling onto him, as my lungs constrict making it hard to breathe. Another tear escapes, and the sound of my name on his lips only makes them come harder. The pure uncertainty...and the fear tipped in at the edge as he calls out to me...

"Trudy?"

18

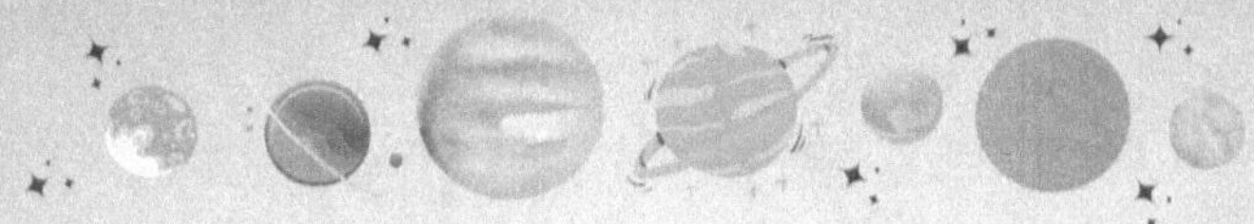

Qhenno

I have done something terribly wrong.

Trudy's shaking above me, her eyes wide as she stares at me with water dripping from her eyes.

"Trudy?"

At the sound of her name, her body jerks with a sob.

"Trudy…show me where…." It hurts for me to speak. That I have harmed her makes my chest ache.

I tried to be gentle, but she is small, that tight little hole between her legs even smaller and tighter than I expected it to be. It was hard to maintain control, but I even resisted the burning urge to sink my fangs into her neck.

Still, I must have pushed too hard.

"Show me where it hurts…" I push past the lump growing in my throat. "I will try to ease your pain."

Qef…I don't know how I'll do that. I have no pain blockers in my trou. Everything is on my ship.

As warm fluid runs down my thighs, another part inside me constricts.

This whole time, I had thought it was her slick running between us...

If it is her lifeblood instead...

She grips my shoulder, her fingers digging into my skin as her body quakes. More water filling her eyes.

"I-I'm sorry." She sniffles and wipes the back of her hand across her eyes and cheeks, making them grow red. "I can't stop."

She sounds annoyed, angry with herself, and alarm goes through me when she repeats the action, making her face redder in her desperation to wipe her face dry.

Grasping her wrist, I force her to stop and her watery eyes find mine.

"I swear I don't cry like this all the time," she says, and then she does the strangest thing. She releases a sad chuckle. "I don't know what it is about you that makes me do this."

"Tell me how to fix this."

She releases another one of those sad chuckles and sniffles again, but at least the water flowing from her eyes has slowed down.

"It's not you. It's..." She shakes her head, turning her gaze away from me. "It's stupid."

Something still feels uneasy inside me and I gaze at her, desperate for her to meet my eyes once more. But she doesn't. She stares off into the dirt as if refusing to look my way.

"Tell me," I whisper.

Closing her eyes for a moment, her throat moves, but she still doesn't look my way.

"What do you know of Lower Earth...or New Earth in general?"

My brows furrow slightly.

I know not much about her world. Only brief scans I looked at while piloting the Zarzenius on our first visit to her world.

"It is a small planet. Once filled with vast oceans and forests...clean air...various species..."

A sad sort of smile graces her lips as she sniffles and nods.

"Yea...but it's nothing like that now. Now it's...filled with metal towers that block the sun and the air is filled with rust. At least...if you live where I do. *Did*. Lower Earth is all I've ever known."

I study her, trying to find a clue as to where she's going with this.

"Lower Earth," I say, my mind going back to those first days when we discovered her species was compatible with ours. "We have heard of the Lower Levels. We have not seen them. Your Earth leaders…they…"

"Kept you up top." Her gaze moves to me. "On the Upper Levels. Where the sun still shines and their gigantic domes are filled with fresh filtered air. They didn't show you Lower Earth because there's nothing to see down there but…desolation…desperation…no hope… Nothing good comes from there…"

She swallows, a stray tear sliding slowly down her cheeks and I get the sense that's something she's been told.

I don't even breathe. I sense this is important…and she is my mate. I want to hear every word she wishes to share with me.

"I'm from the Lower Levels." She releases a breath. "We…don't get to…most of us don't get to experience…*this*. I never imagined I would ever experience this."

Her gaze moves up to the flendrils still circling us. Their light plays against the cave walls even though most of them have returned to their resting places on the roof.

"Flendrils?" I ask.

Trudy chuckles, her gaze warming as she looks at me, even though another tear releases from her eye and runs down her cheek. Letting go of one of her hands, I lift my finger to it and brush it from her cheek.

"Not flendrils," she says, her voice gone soft. "*This*. What we just shared."

I pause, waiting for her to continue.

"I know this is silly. It doesn't matter to you either way and I really shouldn't be laying all of my feelings on the floor. It certainly isn't the sort of thing a girl's supposed to do on a first date."

My brows furrow. She's said a few things that I don't understand.

I brush another tear from her cheek.

"My ari, nothing you say or feel is witless. And *everything* that concerns you is my business."

She sniffles again, her mouth turning down as she tries to smile. It makes me pull her into me and she buries her face into my neck.

I was so worried about being worthy of her...I didn't realize she needed me in this way. That she's been fighting to remain strong, all the while battling monsters that have been trying to bring her down.

Holding her close, I let her body sink into mine. I won't let her go.

"Your life on New Earth...it sounds like it was filled with obstacles."

"It was...but there were some good times too..."

My brows furrow slightly. The world she comes from seems horrible. Like Atar was, before the revolution. "I do not understand why your world has not made life easier for females, males even, who experience difficulty..."

"They used to," she says, "Way back, hundreds of years ago. The humans back then tried to combine society. There were no levels..."

"What happened?"

Trudy sighs. "Some say it was the world war...that the balance of power shifted and society broke down. Those with power didn't want to spend scarce resources caring for those who couldn't contribute as much as others. Eventually, the world split in two. The rich built on top of us, leaving us to rot on the ground."

I feel the burden she's been made to carry, almost as if it is my own.

"Give me your pain," I say into her still-damp tendrils. "Give me your sorrow. I am here. You are no longer alone."

Trudy shudders against me and sniffles. I can almost feel some of the strain leave her body.

"Why are you so *nice*?" she says after a few moments.

I release a soft chuckle. "I'm not. At least, Bhihan would say I'm not."

"Bhihan?"

"My brother in arms. He fights alongside me when we go on missions with the prince."

"Prince?" She tries to force her head up, but the pressure of my hand at the base of her neck keeps her head down.

A laugh huffs through my nose. "You will meet him soon."

"Okay..." she says. "Is he looking for a mate too?"

A growl immediately leaves my lips. "Yes, but he can't have you."

Trudy nuzzles further into me. "Why's that?"

"Because *you're mine*."

When she burrows deeper into me, I know she doesn't care about Bhihan or the prince. She only wanted me to say it out loud.

It makes my insides quiver and melt.

"Most people where I come from don't get to have mates. We don't marry. A lot don't have kids. Most are outlawed from doing so." She inhales deeply and sighs. "I have been alone for so long, I accepted that way of life. But you...you've..."

When she sniffles again, I know her eye waters are back and I grip her to me, not sure of what to do.

If it was Aqnar, second in command, he would know what to do. Even Bhihan might know what to do. But I, who have read every info tab on mating, am flummoxed now that I have my mate in my arms.

"We're treated like we're trash. Like we're nothing. That we aren't...*deserving*. Lower Earth..."

"Is the place that has made you so strong."

Trudy sniffles. "What?"

"Do you realize what you have been through, my mate?" Even thinking about it makes my insides roil with pain, anger, and sorrow.

Trudy sniffles again but I know she is listening to my every word.

"The first time I laid eyes on you, you were fighting."

She releases a huff through her nose. "I...I'm glad that's what you think. I was at the point of curling into a ball and just...giving up..."

"But you didn't." I ease back, turning my head so I can see her face. "I know many Atari females who could not have endured what you have and survived." My gaze moves over her face as she grows silent, warmth building in her eyes as she watches me. "My mate...you are incredible. More than I could have ever asked for."

When our eyes meet, something passes in Trudy's gaze that I can't decipher.

"How are you so sure? We just met, how can you...*feel* so much for me already. I mean...I...like you." Her cheeks increase in redness as she licks her lips. "What's not to like?"

She likes me.

A low purr begins in my chest, one I can't control as my shaft lengthens and hardens within her once more.

Trudy inhales loud enough for me to hear, her eyes glazing over as her lashes fall to her cheeks.

"But I don't get it…"

"When I mark you, you will. You will understand the bond, because you will feel it too."

Her bottom lip disappears into her mouth as her breaths increase, and when I adjust her on me, giving her a shallow thrust in the process, she whimpers, shivers going through her frame.

"When will you mark me?" she whispers, glazed eyes peeking at me.

Brushing away a lock of her hair, my fingers caress her cheek, my thumb brushing over her lips.

"Only when you want me to."

The feel of her lips underneath my thumb only makes me harder and my cock pulses within her warm sheath.

Trudy gasps a little, her cheeks growing even warmer.

When she lifts a hand and grasps my thumb, shivers go down my arm. As she guides my thumb into her mouth, I can almost feel my eyes bleed to black.

"Trudy…" I growl.

"Again," she whispers.

<h1 style="text-align:center">19</h1>

Trudy

I've poured out my heart to this male. *Twice*! Something I never do with anyone. *Ever*.

I don't know what it is about him, but he…he feels like someone I've known all my life.

And this mate thing…if I had to spend the rest of my life with a male like him, I…I could. God knows I could.

As Qhenno grips me and rolls to his side, flipping us so I'm underneath him, I'm given the most exquisite view.

The muscles in his chest are hard underneath his damp skin. He breathes in deep as he looks down at me, those dark eyes taking me in as if he wants to devour me.

He adjusts my legs, lifting them so they straddle his hips as he gazes down at me.

I wonder what he sees…

A growl rumbles in his chest as he pulls out, that hard cock of his sliding through my slick channel as if he made a path for it to fit inside me. When that flared tip makes an obscene pop as it leaves my entrance, Qhenno releases another low rumble in his chest.

Those fangs of his appear and he swipes a tongue over them.

Looking at him, everything inside me quivers.

Balancing my legs on his arms, Qhenno reaches down to hook a finger into the waist of my panties. In one movement, he pulls them over my hips, ripping them in two. They fall to the side as pieces of useless cloth.

"Are you tired?" he growls.

"Tired?"

"How strong are your arms?"

My brows furrow with slight confusion.

He growls again. "Doesn't matter. I will support you."

With that, he pulls me up against his chest, my naked ass nestled on his pecs as my whole body is suspended upside down. A surprised yelp leaves my throat just as I choke on a moan that suddenly barrels through me.

Something hot and wet closes over my entire pussy, making me quiver.

"Qef me," Qhenno growls, his words muffled as his tongue swipes through my folds.

"Oh—!" I pant. The sensation is so unexpected, my eyes roll over as I try to brace my arms on the ground beneath us.

Qhenno lifts me higher, both arms wrapping around the curve of my ass as he full-on buries his face between my thighs.

"Haa—"

He takes my clit into his mouth, groaning as he sucks on it as if he's trying to milk it for cum.

"Qef," his groan rumbles into my pussy like the business end of a vibrator, right before he buries his face deeper, eliciting a strangled moan from my throat as his tongue finds its way deep inside me.

"Qhenno!" I gasp.

All I receive is a rumble of pleasure. One that makes slick gather deep inside my cunt and causes me to shudder.

"Mm," Qhenno rumbles, before his tongue slips from within me. Adjusting himself, he grips my ass with only one arm supporting me as the other brushes over my clit.

He spreads me open with those fingers, a rumble of approval going through his chest as he stares down at the little throbbing bud at my center.

"So beautiful," he whispers.

I want to answer. I want to say something. All that happens is my eyes rolling over once more as two of his fingers dip into me, thrusting as his mouth closes over my clit once more.

I shudder and jerk, unable to control myself. My mouth opens to warn him I'm about to reach my peak but all that comes out is a loud moan.

My pussy clenches on his fingers making him growl once more with approval as he lips and swipes at my tenderness, taking every shudder, every moan, and making me want more.

Finally slipping his fingers from inside me, Qhenno slides me down his chest, leaving a trail of slick and wetness down his pecs as he positions me in his lap.

My chest heaves as I look at him.

I can feel the heat in my cheeks. The same heat that's radiating through me...and probably him too.

That hard, hot rod pokes against me. Nestled in the valley between my butt, it feels even bigger than before as it throbs.

"Do you want me, my mate?" he asks.

I nod, not trusting my voice.

"Do you want me in that tight little hole of yours?"

"Yes," I pant.

Qhenno growls and lifts me enough to position himself at my entrance. Another rumble goes through him as he tilts his forehead to mine.

"So qeffing small. I'm afraid I will break you."

I grasp his jaw and tilt my head so I can brush my lips against his. "You won't."

He pauses for only a moment before he guides himself to my entrance, teeth grit as he pushes that flared head against me.

"Let me in..." he whispers.

Groans rumble, echoing through the cave when he finally pops in.

"Qhenno..." I breathe.

"My ari," he says, rocking his hips in slow, measured movements.

Gripping me to him, he watches me as his movements grow faster, those pumps sending his thick shaft deeper and deeper inside me till I can no longer keep my eyes open.

"Trudy," he growls, making my eyes flicker open.

A surprising shock of pleasure goes through me when I see his face.

He looks…possessed like he was before. Only now he's inside me, and I can feel every inch of his need.

"Mark me, Qhenno."

Qhenno growls so loud, the water butterflies skitter off the walls again.

"Don't tempt me with such words, my ari. My control is not the best. Not with your softness wrapped around me. Not when you smell and taste so good… Not when you *feel* so good."

Even as he says the words, his fangs protrude. Something like water, or maybe saliva, drips from them to slide down his lips and he swipes his tongue over it.

With one hard thrust, he buries himself deep inside me and I cry out, gripping on to his shoulders.

Leaning in close, Qhenno runs his tongue over my cheek before whispering in my ear.

"If I bite you now, my ari…I will never let you go."

His words send delicious shivers through my skin.

"Bite me?" I whisper back.

Qhenno pulls back almost torturously slowly before sliding all the way in again, rumbling with every inch that he seats inside me.

"Right here," he says, dipping his head and grazing his fangs over my neck. I shiver again.

"This is not good, my ari. Now the thought is in my head," he whispers, pulling back to thrust deep inside me again.

His tongue flicks out, traveling over my skin.

"Please," I whisper.

I want it.

If there is a bond, I want to feel it.

If he is my destiny, I want him now. All of him. *Everything*.

Qhenno growls, a shudder going through him as his slow thrusts torture us both.

He shakes his head, a groan going through him as if resisting is painful.

"You have to want it…after I bite you, there is no turning back."

I touch his jaw, my gaze meeting his. "It's not the bite I want," I whisper. "It's you."

Qhenno stops moving, his gaze engulfing me before he suddenly closes his lips over mine.

A moan goes through me, one that disappears into his mouth as his tongue dives against mine.

I feel as we tilt, as he bears down, his hips pounding into me till I am shaking on his cock.

"Trudy," he growls, breaking the kiss as his lips move to my neck. He breathes my name again over my skin as his hips begin to piston within me.

Euphoria. This can only be euphoria. Because I can't feel my limbs…myself…my body. All I can feel is a river of pleasure flowing through me, the current crashing through my frame to culminate at the center of my thighs.

"Qhenno!" I breathe his name the moment I feel the prick against my skin.

It comes with pain, as his fangs enter my neck. Pain that's almost immediately erased by ecstasy.

A scream leaves my lips as an orgasm crashes through me.

I grip on to him, my mate, as my body trembles against his, and as he pistons into me, his fangs still in my neck, he lets out a rumble of his own.

But his thrusts don't cease.

He readjusts himself, going back on his haunches and taking me with him as he continues to pummel into me and when he stiffens, warmth flooding me from the inside as his cock twitches, he finally extracts his fangs from my skin.

I'm panting, gripping on to him as he licks the wound, murmuring words in a language I cannot understand as he licks and kisses me.

"You are mine, my ari. Now and forever."

20

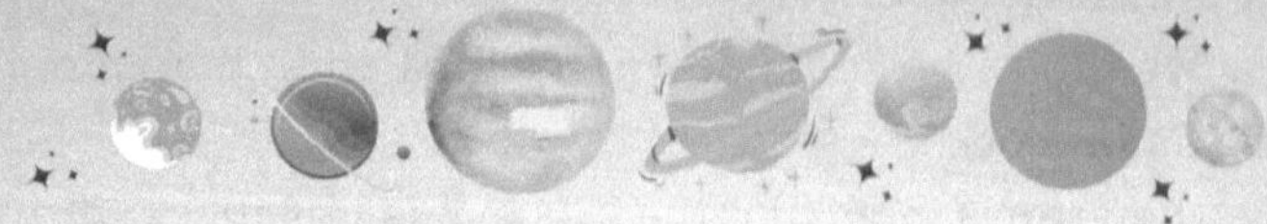

Qhenno

My mate is sleeping. Nestled on top of my trou, her now-dry clothes thrown over her to keep her warm, she looks peaceful and…sated.

So why am I pacing, making a path so deep I might divert the river flowing beside us?

The tight skin at the back of my neck pulses and I run a hand over it. It's not as hot as before. Not as tense.

That's only because I marked Trudy. Bit her and released all the life spirit that had been gathering in my fangs.

I did everything I read I should do.

Mark your mate. Release your life spirit. Solidify the bond.

My life organ thunders in my chest with my unease and I pace again.

A few flendrils leave their spot on the cave wall and fly down the river, following its path into the darkness until it breaks through the cave and into the open world once more.

We will have to follow them and leave soon. Night creatures, the flendrils will all leave to feed in the dark cycle. And…we cannot stay in this small cavern for much longer. No one was insane enough to jump off and follow us, but I am sure the Morang know this river exists here. After the slaves escape, they will check it.

With the star taking its rest, I should be able to get us to my shuttle by sticking to the shadows.

If the Morang believe we have perished, it would be for the best.

But it isn't the second phase of our escape that has me nervous.

Rubbing that area at the back of my neck, I stop pacing to gaze at my mate once more.

She fell asleep within moments of my injecting my life spirit inside her and she hasn't woken since.

I reckon it has been at least three yoras.

Worry crawls up my spine.

I have no instruments to check her life force…and the bond…it has not awakened yet. I expected to feel it bloom the moment my life spirit entered her veins.

I was wrong.

I am still the holder of an unattached cord. My connection to her has not grown stronger.

I crouch over her, my finger brushing against her cheek. She hardly responds, and more worry grows.

Aqnar, our second in command, was the first to locate one of the humans. She turned out to be his mate. The fates led him directly to her…and when he marked her…he almost killed her.

My mate is also human.

What if…

I shake the thought away.

The only reason Aqnar almost failed was because his mate had an implant that interfered with the bond's creation.

Trudy told me she doesn't have such an implant. There should be nothing impeding us.

But now I wonder if she was wrong. Her world leaders have been untrustworthy. What if they did something to her…put that implant inside her…without her being aware.

"Trudy," I whisper, and a soft moan leaves her lips, one that has my cock hardening and rising against my leg, even though we mated not long ago.

One of Trudy's eyes flickers open and she stares my way as if not seeing me.

"Trudy?"

She rises on her arms then, squinting as she looks my way.

A groan leaves her lips.

"How long have I been sleeping?"

Leaning closer, I brush my forehead against hers, and she smiles up at me. "Not long."

She smiles at me, but my worried gaze searches her features for any sign that *something* is happening.

When her fingers rise to skirt over the spot where I sunk my fangs into her neck, I hold my breath.

"How do you feel?" I can't help the expectancy that's in my voice. The anticipation. That tinge of fear.

By the gods, I have been fighting wars all my life and not even my enemies have this power to bring me to my knees as she does.

"I feel…" she begins, her brows furrowing as she continues rubbing her neck. "Hot." She huffs a laugh through her nose as her gaze rises to mine. "Like I'm burning up."

Well…that's certainly better than feeling nothing at all. Though… the warmth rising in her body could just be the beginning of a fever from the icy cold water that I took her through.

Thinking about it now, my head turns as I watch the river rushing by.

"Is it just me…" Trudy whispers, "or is it…darker in here?"

"Darker," I answer. "The flendrils are leaving to feed. They will no longer bless us with their light."

A beat passes between us before her fingers brush against my jaw. They are warm. Warmer than they've been every other time she's touched me.

My life-organ skips a beat with more anticipation. Possibly, this is how the bond forms in her kind. Warmth, like the one that burns at the nape of my neck, but spread throughout her body instead?

I can only hope.

Leaning forward, I press my lips against hers, enjoying the feel of her hot tongue as it meets mine.

But when I reach forward and grasp her shoulders, the heat within her body is startling. Startling enough that I pull away, my eyes widening as I stare at her.

"What?" she whispers.

"Your temperature…"

Her cheeks look even rosier in the few minutes that she's awakened. "Yea…I do feel hot. Is this because you bit me?"

Worry furrows my brow and I glance at the water rushing behind us again.

I want to tell her everything will be fine. But…I do not know that as truth.

"We need to get back to the Zarzenius," I finally say. I need her on the ship in case anything happens. I cannot risk her health declining without a med bay at our disposal.

"Your mother ship?"

"Aye."

Trudy releases a slow breath. "How?"

I turn my gaze back to her. "The river."

Trudy

Qhenno seems tense.

Maybe after what we shared I feel closer to him and can read him better, but as he helps me get dressed, sliding my trousers over my legs without me having to ask for his help, an air of worry wafts from him.

Shrugging on my blouse, I search within myself for something new.

Something powerful that will let me know that I'm now mated.

All I feel is…heat. My body is burning up. Even the breaths that come from my nose are scorching.

Hot.

And *horny*.

No matter how I try to fight the feeling, from the moment I woke up and saw him close, my body's been calling for his touch.

Is this the bond?

Is this what he constantly feels for me? An overwhelming urge to pin me down and fuck my brains out? Because that's what I'm feeling for him. And I'm not so sure that's all it should be.

Is that why he's tense? Maybe the whole biting thing didn't work?

Brushing my fingers against the spot that he bit, I only feel the faintest twinge of discomfort. The wound's already healing.

As Qhenno pulls on his trou, I glance up at him and his gaze is focused on the trousers. That tension radiates from him. Unease.

Both now ready, he pauses and finally lifts his gaze to mine.

"Are you worried about the river?" *Or me?* I want to ask, but somehow, my tongue twists and I can't say the words.

"Our first introduction to the water didn't go well," he murmurs, brushing a hand against my cheek.

"I'm better prepared this time." I smile as well as I can at him.

The truth is...I am terrified of going back into that water. The feeling of my lungs bursting is fresh in my mind. But I can't back out. That water is the only way out of this nightmare. I have to do it.

As Qhenno reaches down and lifts me into his arms, I don't complain. He grips me close to him, checks that his communicator device is secure in his trou, and takes his first few steps down into the icy water.

His chest heaves against me and when I look up at him, his eyes are a startling golden mix of honey and warmth.

"Hold your breath, my ari," he says, before he slowly dips his lips to mine.

His kiss is sweet, promising, and I almost forget to do as he says and hold my breath.

When we dip under the water, it feels as if it sizzles against my hot skin. It's fast, the current. Faster than before. And I can't tell if we are moving quickly or if it's the water that's pushing us.

Eyes shut tight, I try not to focus on the breath stuck in my lungs. I grip on to Qhenno and I focus on the way his arms feel sure and strong.

Flicking my lids open, I'm surprised to see light all around us. My eyes widen as the little water butterflies swim alongside us, all heading in the same direction like one glow-in-the-dark unit.

Qhenno looks down at me and his gaze says it all. I'm rendered speechless as I look up at him.

The way he's looking at me…

It's as if time has stopped and I'm in a magical land with someone who…actually cares about me.

My heart swells…and with it, the immediate urge to pull my trousers down and slide over his cock.

The thought hits me so suddenly, I moan into his mouth and Qhenno's brows furrow slightly, concern in his gaze before he has to focus back on where he's taking me.

Oh my God…

My clit pulses, the icy water doing absolutely nothing to dampen the heat growing between my thighs. I gasp into his mouth when a surge hits me so hard, I jerk in his arms.

It's so strong. I've never felt anything like it before.

I need…I need to fuck him.

Now.

Right here. In the fucking freezing torrent.

Qhenno's wide gaze meets mine once more and worry seeps into his gaze.

This is it, isn't it? This has to be because of the bond. The bite. This is because he bit me.

I have never before in my entire life wanted to grind my pussy against a male the way I want to fuck him right now.

I can't help myself. My tongue moves on its own as it dips into his mouth.

Qhenno's eyes widen some more before a groan rumbles into my mouth and fuck me if it doesn't make my body react in the most obscene way. Even in the icy water, I can feel the slick gather between my legs.

Qhenno surges upward and we break the surface. Ripping his lips from mine, he inhales deeply, his eyes on me.

"Trudy?"

I'm breathing hard too, but not for the urge to pull air into my lungs, but for the burning need that's quickly taking control of me.

"Say something, my ari."

I'm distantly aware that the urge to pull large amounts of air into my lungs isn't there. All I can focus on is the feel of his strong arms around me.

He's walking out of the water and, for a moment, my gaze slips to the dark night around us. Distant lights twinkle and, above us, stars fill the night sky.

We are out in the open.

We did it?

No. *He* did it.

It's hard to swallow as my gaze falls back on the male holding me. Qhenno. The man I want to fuck so badly, my nipples are hardening with every breath.

My mate.

The thought registers so hard that I inhale sharply.

It feels like my heart swells and then constricts suddenly, the muscle itself bending and stretching out of myself toward him, like a cord that needs to be bound to another.

A heartbeat thumps in my ears and my eyes widen slightly.

I'm pretty sure it wasn't mine.

Qhenno staggers to a stop, his brows furrowing as he stares ahead. His chest heaves, creating a gentle sway, as he stands holding me in the night.

"Qhenno?" I whisper, licking my lips at the sound of his name on my tongue.

When he slowly brings his gaze to mine, the swirl of emotions in his eyes makes that cord within me pulse and tremble.

"Qhenno…" I breathe.

A breath shudders through his nose as he dips his lips to mine. I moan, unable to stop the sweet pulse of need that's making that little bud between my folds swell and throb.

"My ari…" Qhenno groans against my lips. "I can feel it." Another breath shudders from him, all the tension that had been gathering in his frame releasing in that single breath.

He was worried.

He was worried about it not working.

I smile against his lips, enjoying the feel of his tongue against mine when he suddenly stiffens.

No, don't stop now.

But when he pulls away from me, his gaze hardening, I know something is amiss.

I hear the sounds shortly after. Gruff voices. Voices I never wanted to hear again.

The Morang.

Qhenno moves quickly, ducking behind some rocks along what seems to be the shore of the raging river.

For the first time since coming from the depths of the frigid water, my gaze lifts and I look around.

The shore is craggy, shadows forming on the large rocks, but despite the unevenness of the terrain, there aren't many places to hide.

"There he is!" one of the Morang shout and Qhenno curses under his breath. Fear cuts through the need surging through me.

They only saw him because he's protecting me, tucking me inside the shadow of the rock instead of hiding himself.

He grips my chin, his touch gentle but insistent as he turns me to face him.

"Stay here. Don't make a sound."

I nod, my chin jerking like I'm having a seizure and when he releases me, gently setting me down on the uneven surface, my heart seizes too.

"Qeffing Morang," Qhenno says as he raises his voice.

My eyes widen slightly.

His whole demeanor changes in an instant.

A lopsided grin teases his lips, flashing the corner of one fang, and his gaze is cold and uncaring.

"I should have expected you would find me," he says, walking away from where he left me.

I want to shift closer so I can see what's going on behind the rock but fear holds me rigid.

The Morang grunt. "You qeffing malapert kit," one of them says.

"Did you think you would get away with what you have done?"

another asks. "The mine is destroyed. All the slaves are gone. Our brethren lay dead at our feet."

Qhenno chuckles. "Ah," he says, "it's been a good day."

There's a snarl and I wonder just how many of them are there. They're so close, I can almost smell them, or maybe it's just the scent of my fear.

"Surprising you even survived the icy current," another says. "We expected to see your lifeless body floating downstream..." He makes a grunt in his throat. "That would have been fun...but this is better. Now we get to skin you alive."

A cry of surprise and fear almost escapes my lips and I have to slam a hand over my mouth. I don't even breathe as I continue listening.

"Why bother?" Qhenno asks. He doesn't even seem mildly concerned with their threat. "We Atari have no war with you, Morang."

"You took a slave with you," the Morang growls so loudly, I feel it in my bones. "And you killed our leader! No one takes from the Morang without punishment!"

Qhenno huffs a laugh through his nose, as if their threat means nothing, and my eyes widen some more.

I completely forgot he is insane!

From what it sounds like, they outnumber him. And those Morang are big motherfuckers.

Shit.

This isn't good. This isn't good at all. After everything we've been through, there is no way Qhenno is at his top strength.

"If you want the female so badly," Qhenno says, "you can have her."

What? My world stutters and stalls, my bones going cold. The only thing that keeps me grounded is that cord that feels wrapped around my heart.

It grows warm and almost feels like it pulses as I focus on it. I feel Qhenno's heartbeat...or rather...I sense it. I sense it and his warmth. They're a stark contrast to the coldness of his words.

"She's in the cave underneath the mountain," he says, and I bite my lip while listening to him. "Go get her if you want."

One of the Morang grunts. "You think we can't scent her on you?" He inhales loud enough that I hear.

"It would be silly if you didn't...wouldn't it?" Qhenno replies, his voice cool and unbothered. "I jumped with her in my arms, hoping she would help soften my fall."

I swallow hard. I don't know where he's getting this bravado from, but my bones are shivering so much, my skeleton will soon start clacking and making noise.

"She's in the cave," Qhenno says, an air of disinterest in his tone that makes my heart ache even though I know he's lying for my sake.

Once more, a flood of warmth comes through that cord wound around my heart and I hang on to it like it's a lifeline.

"I do not believe you left her there," one of the Morang says.

"She wasn't much use to me," Qhenno says, his voice hardening even though that pulse of warmth coming through the bond is sure.

One of the Morang laugh. "Fool. She is a broken female. One the Khuru sold to us for just a few credits. You should have noticed that before you escaped with her."

Another snorts. "Must have only realized when the useless thing couldn't move. The only thing a female like that is good for is—"

He doesn't get to finish. His words are immediately cut off by the sound of a fist hitting flesh.

Qhenno roars and I peek from behind the rock to see him launched into the air, his fist extended as it lands into the Morang's jaw.

There are three of them, all wounded by the looks of it, but the other two move immediately. But Qhenno is fast. Much faster than he was the first time I saw him in that club, and I realize now that he hadn't been giving it his all back then.

He spins, evading the thrust of one of the Morangs' spears. The Morang adjusts himself, charging forward as his colleague from the side does the same. Qhenno kicks out, catching one of them in the wrist and their spear flies in the air and clatters over the rocks, falling right into my lap.

My heart gives a huge thump.

"Oh no. Oh no no no no no."

The owner of this spear is going to come for it and then what?

I grip the weapon, tempted to throw it far away from me, but one more peek at the fight and I end up only holding on to it.

In the few seconds of the spear falling on me, Qhenno has taken down one of the Morang but the others are still attacking, although one seems even more wounded than before.

He focuses on that one, driving kicks into the Morang's chest, but the fucker only staggers backward, coming in my direction.

Fuck!

With one flying kick, Qhenno lands a blow on Morang's head. It twists, almost breaking in its socket, but the beast manages to stagger and fall on his back.

Gripping the spear, my wide eyes are glued to him. He's fallen enough that he can see me and when his head turns and his gaze lands on me, my veins shrivel and grow cold.

Fuck.

Busy with the other one, Qhenno grabs the spear of the other fallen Morang and charges at the one still standing. They fight, both skilled with the weapon. Neither landing any blows. Both blocking and doing a good job at it.

I swallow hard, my gaze falling back on the Morang that had his eyes on me.

He's still staring at me but then his gaze flicks to something on the ground between us.

My eyes follow his to see something dark and unnatural lying in the dirt. I'm no arms dealer, but that thing is obviously a gun. It must have fallen when he did.

He stretches for it but can't reach and is too wounded to just get up and grab it.

My heart thumps as my gaze darts back at Qhenno. There's a nasty cut across his chest and even though he's managing to keep that one Morang from landing any finishing blows, he's obviously playing defense.

I have to help him.

Measuring the distance between me and the gun, it's about an equal distance from me as it is to the Morang reaching for it.

I could get there first.

I don't allow that little voice of fear to stop me from moving, because the moment I brace on my arms and begin pulling myself across the rocky ground, it begins screaming at me at full force.

What the hell am I doing?

I should keep hiding. I should try to go away from the fight, not towards it.

But when I look in Qhenno's direction and see him fighting for both of our lives, my heart swells. For *him*.

I don't want to lose…*him*. Qhenno.

It's a realization that makes my heart swell and I pause, seconds passing by as I lock eyes with the Morang still reaching for the gun.

My heart is like a bongo drum on steroids as I hold the Morang's gaze while moving closer. For a moment, he sneers as if he thinks I am trying to save myself and run away. But when I continue moving in his direction, his face slowly morphs into utter rage the moment he realizes I'm not running away…I'm coming toward him.

He stretches for the gun again, grunting as he flips on his belly and tries to grab it.

My heart thumps and fear makes me shudder but I keep moving forward anyway. The Morang in front of me calls out to his companion, but focused on Qhenno, he doesn't seem to hear.

My fingers close over the gun at the same moment that the Morang's does.

He growls, his sharp teeth flashing at me, and I swallow hard.

For how long have I feared even looking at them while in that mine? Back then, when those same sharp teeth would snap at other unfortunate souls like myself.

Well, I'm not so unfortunate now. I've got someone fighting in my corner and I'll be damned if I let these crooks take away the one good thing that's come out of all this shit.

When the Morang tugs on the gun, if it had been the old me, he would've probably been able to pull it from my grasp. But now, now I hold on to it as if my life depends on it. And it probably does.

The Morang pulls so hard, I slide across the rocky ground and I hiss as pain shoots across my skin.

I can't win like this, but I'm not empty-handed. In my other hand, I have the spear that had fallen. I didn't let go of it.

The moment we both realize I still have the spear is clear. The Morang's eyes widen and I sneer as I lift the spear. The sharp metal glints in the starlight as I lift the weapon and slam the pointed end into the Morang's arm.

He roars, releasing the gun and drawing the attention of his colleague that's fighting Qhenno.

It's all Qhenno needs. The distraction is enough for him to bury his spear into the other Morang's chest. The beast roars and staggers back before colliding with a rock.

I watch him fall, my heart thumping before I realize that Qhenno is suddenly right before me.

He grips me to him so tightly it is hard to breathe. Pressing my face to his chest, he mutters words in that tongue that I can't understand before he peppers kisses into my hair.

"My ari," he whispers into my hair. "My brave, perfect little ari."

I try to push him away so I can look at the wound on his chest, but he won't let me.

"Qhenno, you're bleeding." I can feel it against my hand. His chest seems soaked with his own blood and now that the obvious danger has been taken care of, a new fear is unlocked in my mind. "Let me see it. You're bleeding pretty badly. We should bandage it or something."

Pushing against him once more, I try to shrug myself out of my blouse. We can use what's left of it to stop his wound from bleeding so much. But when Qhenno finally releases me, it's not to let me tend to him. He pulls the spear from the Morang that I wounded and buries the blade into the Morang's neck. Moving to the other wounded one, he does the same thing till none of them are moving.

Then and only then, does he return to me, take me into his arms, and begin walking into the darkness.

"Qhenno?"

"Yes, my ari?" he answers, his gaze focused ahead with a snarl on his face that almost seems permanent. "It is time I take you home."

21

Qhenno

I can feel the bond thrumming between us as strongly as I can feel my life-organ thump in my chest.

Nestled against me, my mate shudders in my embrace, the strain of the past few moments seeping from her frame.

Those qeffing Morang.

Seeing them come so close to taking her away from me opened another level of rage mixed in with fear I never knew existed within me.

I need to take Trudy home. I need her off this planet and back on Atar where she will be safe in my lodging, surrounded by soft furs and comfort and not the dangers this world has sent her way.

"Qhenno." Her voice rings through my thoughts and when I glance down at her, something inside me softens. She is so delicate and warm. That heat radiating from her spreads through my entire being and dulls the pain in my chest.

"Qhenno, we need to stop. You're bleeding. *Badly.*" There's distress in her voice and I am sorry I am the cause.

"I am fine," I say to her. "I will be well."

"But *I'm* not!" she retorts. "You're losing a lot of blood and it's freaking me out. We need to stop. Please, just put me down somewhere and we can look at it."

Her worry makes me feel…warm. As we near my shuttle, my lips twist into a smile.

"When we get inside, I will let you tend to me, if that will ease your fears."

"Inside?"

Since I took her into my arms and walked away from the carnage, her eyes have been on me. She has not looked where we are going, not looked at the wounds I can see on her arms from when she crawled across the rocks to my aid.

She's been focused on *me* and as the bond thrums between us, the heat of her body warming mine, I know that the fates have finally bestowed upon me the greatest gift.

Even in the mine shaft, before she knew she was my mate, she cared about my wounds.

A smile passes over my lips.

She thinks she *likes* me…I think it is deeper than that. Even before I marked her.

Trudy finally turns her gaze to our surroundings, her eyes squinting ahead.

Dark metal glinting in the low light of the stars, my ship lies hidden far from the Morang mine.

As we approach it now, it interacts with the communicator and the door opens at the same time as Trudy's mouth does.

"Your ship…" she breathes.

I grunt, dipping my head to the soft strands of her hair and inhaling deeply. "Yes." I can finally take her home now.

As I climb into the vessel and it shuts behind me, I tell the onboard computer to prepare for liftoff—destination the Zarzenius.

"Destination accepted," an automated female voice says.

The engines hum almost immediately, and I feel my mate's pulse increase.

Dipping my nose to her head once more, I release a low purr.

"Don't be afraid. You are safe now."

Trudy shakes her head, a surprised sort of laugh huffing through her nose. "I'm not scared...I'm just...is this real? Are we really leaving this place?"

"Yes, and not a moment too soon."

She releases another huff of laughter through her nose as I move to the back of the shuttle and set her down on the raised sleeping area there.

She eases up on her elbows immediately, her eyes returning to my chest.

"Oh my God..." She reaches for me without hesitation, her fingers skimming over my chest. Her eyes widen by the second, horror transforming their kind glow as she stares at me. "W-we have to get you stitched up." Those wide eyes lift to mine, more horror seeping into them. "You walked all the way while carrying me...while you looked like *that*?"

"Don't like what you see?" I growl softly. The stark white lights of the shuttle's interior only highlight her beauty...and now that we are no longer in danger, something else stirs inside me, dispelling the fury and fear of our recent encounter with the Morang.

Trudy's lips twist, her gaze softening only a little as she smiles. Her cheeks warm but then her lips tighten and her eyes become pointed as she glares at me.

"I love what I'm seeing apart from the fact that you're still losing blood." Her gaze darts behind me. "Where's the first aid kit?"

Before I can tell her, she's already shuffling off the sleeping platform.

I grip her arm lightly, stopping her as I reach above us and take the first aid kit off the wall.

The engines roar, finally firing up to full power as the shuttle lifts into the air.

Bracing a hand on the wall behind her, I hand Trudy the first aid kit, watching as she gulps, her eyes widening slightly as she listens to the ship.

When we pick up speed, she gulps again and hurriedly empties the contents of the kit on the platform beside her.

"Um...I don't know what any of these things are." Her gaze darts to mine. I shrug and brace another arm overhead, caging her in. Now that it is calm, the bond thrums between us even stronger.

I wonder if she can feel it. Because watching her dig through all the items thrown beside her, worrying about me, is causing the strangest reaction.

My cock stirs and grows, pressing into my trou.

I need my mate.

For what feels like the hundredth time, I almost lost her. I need to drown that feeling with sounds of her little whimpers and moans. I want to hear her scream my name.

"Qhenno, will this do?" She gazes up at me and her mouth slackens slightly. Shaking her head, her cheeks grow rosy the moment we break the atmosphere and gravity control kicks in.

Trudy jerks a little, her body floating for a moment before it falls back to the platform, those mounds on her chest bouncing in a way that makes me want to have them bouncing in my face…or better yet, in my mouth.

A low groan releases from me the moment Trudy begins to dab an antiseptic swab against my chest, wiping away the dried and wet lifeblood gathered there.

She hisses, her gaze darting to mine. "Sorry, I'm trying to be as gentle as I can."

I groan again and she apologizes, unaware that it is the sensation of her fingers on my skin that's causing me to clench my teeth as she works.

As soon as she secures a bandage to my wound, I grab her wrist and push her back onto the platform.

Trudy squeals and it only makes me growl again.

"Careful, I'm not confident I did that well. I don't want you to hurt yourself even more."

"Hurting myself is the least of my concern."

Pinning her arms above her head, I lean down over her.

Trudy whimpers, her lower lip trembling before she pulls it into her mouth.

"I'm not sure you should be touching me right now," she whispers.

I growl, the thought of not touching her utterly unagreeable.

"I'm not feeling so well," she continues.

That makes me pause and I exit my trance for a moment. "What is wrong, my ari?"

"I—" she pants, her cheeks growing rosier. "Every time you touch me...I..."

"Tell me, my ari..."

"I want to fuck your brains out, and it's not normal. I mean, the intensity of it is not normal. I wanted to hump you when we were in the river too, and now that we're no longer in danger... God..."

A groan rumbles through me at her words. They are a sure indicator that she is feeling the need to rut, probably even rivaling mine. It almost makes me go feral with need.

But my mate's arms are red, and possibly countless other places on her body as well.

Relaxing my hold on her arms, I reach for an antiseptic swab and begin tending to the scrapes on her skin, adding bandages to the spots as I go. Trudy shudders with each touch and soon her fist is closed, tightening on the edge of her blouse as if she wants to pull the fibers apart.

When I finally tend to the final wound, she releases a breath.

"Thank the gods, finally." She reaches for me, pulling me down into her embrace as her mouth closes over mine.

I groan, accepting her sweetness as a rumble goes through me.

This isn't like before when we shared each other. This...is different.

There is a hunger burning within her that I've never felt before, one that ignites a fire within me that I don't want to extinguish.

We struggle to get her clothes off, both impatient, and when she lies bare before me, I can hardly stop myself from running my hands over her body.

Panting, Trudy rips at my trou and I somehow manage to slip it off. I kick it off my feet as my cock bounces and pokes down into my mate's soft belly. The thought of my seed filling her...making her belly swell. It makes me groan as she grips my shaft and forces it downwards.

A moment of clarity clears the fog in my brain and I still her hand.

"You're not ready for me yet," I whisper.

"Qhenno, I've never been wetter in my life. I'm practically weeping for you down there." She tugs me lower, her fist tightening around my shaft in a way that makes my fangs extend with need. "I need you," she whimpers. "Now."

As I line up with her entrance, her slick coats my tip, making me growl.

I can't resist when she closes her eyes and uses one hand to spread her soft folds, easing me inside her with the other.

"Qhenno, I'm hot. I'm so hot. I'm burning up and I need you to fuck me. Hard."

I stare down at her, my mind clouding over with her words.

"I can't explain it. It's like I'm sick and your dick is medicine. It doesn't make sense but I know your cock will make me feel better," Trudy pants. "I want you so bad."

When her eyes open to look at me, heat and need deep inside them, I know I'm gone.

"Please," she whispers.

With a growl, I surge forward.

Who am I to make my mate beg?

22

Trudy

There's a crackle in the ship that I don't hear immediately, a moan barreling through me and into the small pillow underneath my face as Qhenno eases inside me, his cock going deep.

Thighs squeezed together between his legs, his hands knead my butt as he slides out, only to thrust forward again.

That flared head of his cock feels like it kisses and sucks on my pussy before it forces its way back into me, and I whimper, another orgasm crashing through me that makes my body jolt and shudder. My nipples rub into the coarse material of the bed and only heighten the sensations rolling through me, and I utter a bunch of gibberish I don't care to know the meaning of.

"—you read?" A voice cuts through the pleasure that's weakening my bones, and I blink my eyes open, turning my head from the center of the pillow so I can breathe.

"Is anyone there? Qef me if this whole operation hasn't gone to the bowels of deepest excrement," the voice continues.

I groan, wondering if Qhenno has fucked my brains out and I'm hearing things. I lost count by the fifth round and no matter how much I've come, I still want more.

He's ruined me for anyone else...but I'm not sure I *want* anyone else.

Not after this.

As Qhenno shudders above me, squeezing my ass as he pulls me into him and fills my womb with spend, he repeats the words he's been saying from the start.

"You're so perfect, my ari," he says before collapsing beside me and pulling me into his arms.

They are words that warm me to my core.

Curling his body around me, our chests heave together as he snuggles into me. So many rounds, and every time, he does the same thing. He snuggles into me right after, holding me close and peppering me with kisses.

I've never felt more...loved...or wanted.

"Qhenno, if you can hear this, you need to contact the Zarzenius immediately," that voice, a male voice, sounds over the speaker in the ship once more.

Qhenno groans. "Ignore him."

Knocked a little out of my daze, I frown, twisting somewhat so I can glance over my shoulder at my mate.

My *mate...*

I can't believe those words are even on my tongue.

"Ignore who? Who is that? Is that your friend on the mother ship?" My heart thumps a little harder. I still can't believe I've made it out of that nightmare at the Morang mine and that I'm on my way to safety and a life with someone I couldn't have expected.

"Bhihan," Qhenno growls, some annoyance in his tone.

"You should answer him ..." I rub the arm that's draped around me and Qhenno huffs and pulls me closer before punching a button overhead.

"I'm here," he growls, his voice so sour I almost laugh at his sudden surliness.

There's another crackle then a string of what sounds like expletives.

"You qeffer. You had me worried. Standard protocol is to send updates back to the Zarzenius. You went silent. I thought the Morang had imprisoned you in one of their mines."

When I glance at Qhenno his gaze warms as he looks at me, a smile gracing his lips.

"Oh Bhihan, I knew you loved me."

The male on the other end growls. "Save such words for the mate you want so badly. Did you find the human?"

"I have her here. We will arrive at the Zarzenius shortly. We are about to go hyper-speed…and then you can have the pleasure of meeting my mate."

The utter pride in his voice makes my heart swell.

"Your what?" the other male says before his end of the line goes silent.

"Speak to you soon, Bhihan…" Qhenno says, lifting his hand to turn off the comms when the other male exclaims what sounds like another curse on the other end of the line.

"What in the qef?!" Bhihan shouts.

"I told you that I was drawn to the mines…" Qhenno begins.

"No, not you. Though, I have to see your mate to believe it is true. But…what in the qef…there's a transport that just jumped from hyper-speed right in front of the Zarzenius."

Qhenno freezes behind me.

"Isn't that dangerous?" I whisper.

"More than dangerous," he replies. "Reckless."

"By the gods…" Bhihan says on the line. "You will not believe what I am seeing."

Rising on his elbows, Qhenno frowns into the roof.

"There's a being…a female?" The male sounds nonplussed, as if the scene before him is too unbelievable to even translate.

"You should hail her, let her know she almost sent you both to your graves with her reckless piloting. Is she the one flying the vessel?"

"I don't think *anyone* is flying the vessel…"

"What?"

Qhenno is fully alert now and so am I.

"She's outside of it, hanging on while…fighting a Darzel." He speaks as if he's not talking to us but relaying the information to himself as he watches the scene unfold. "I can't see her face, but I don't think she's a Darzel herself. Too tall. Too lithe." There's another string of curses. "They're heading right toward us and it looks as if she needs my help."

"Wait, Bhihan—" Qhenno begins.

"I have to go."

The line crackles and dies, leaving me and Qhenno staring at each other.

"Do you think he will be alright?" I ask.

"Bhihan is capable of taking care of himself. I wouldn't worry." Even though he says this, there is a slight furrow to his brow. Resting on his side, he pulls me against him once more, spooning me as he curls around me.

For a few moments, we lay in silence.

"You're worried about him, aren't you," I finally say.

Qhenno makes a sound in his throat. "You can tell?"

I nod. "I can feel it." I move my hand to the center of my chest. "Here."

Qhenno makes a rumbling sound like a purr and places his hand over mine.

"The bond," he says. "I will have to be mindful not to project my feelings through it. I don't want you to worry about me."

I'm already shaking my head. "No, don't you dare. I *like* feeling it. I like feeling *you*."

Qhenno groans, pulling me closer. He buries his face into my hair and kisses me there. "Your temperature has lowered."

I nod. Who knew good cock was a cure for a fever?

As that comfortable silence extends between us, my shoulders sag as I relax.

When was the last time I felt this at peace? I…can't remember.

"I feel it too," Qhenno says after a few moments.

"Feel what?" I whisper.

"I feel the bond." He swallows so hard, I feel his throat move against my scalp where his head rests. "I feel *you*."

My heart thumps at the weight of his words…or maybe the sound of his voice. How heavy it is. Filled with emotion. And I realize at that moment, that all this time, I have not seen him vulnerable.

At least…not in the way I'm used to vulnerability.

Twisting so I can look at him, I lift my hand to his jaw. He tilts his head into my palm, those golden eyes looking down at me with so much feeling in them that my heart swells.

His gaze searches mine as I look up at him, as if there is something still lingering on his chest. But I don't need to stare into his eyes to see it.

I can feel it.

Underneath all the warmth flooding from him to me, there is a note of fear.

"You are not at ease," I whisper.

Qhenno blinks and his throat moves again before he suddenly smiles. It transforms his face and my heart stutters a little. He's breathtaking, this man. And he's mine.

I can hardly believe it.

"I'm going to have to get used to having someone around who can read me so easily," he says, running a hand through his white strands.

"What's bothering you?"

His smile slowly dies, and I watch as some of the light leaves his eyes. He averts his gaze, staring at the wall before us that has a small storage compartment attached to it.

"Docking in fifteen minutes," the shuttle suddenly says. "Please be ready to engage manual controls in case of emergency."

Qhenno releases a breath and I worry he might take the distraction as a way to not answer my question.

But he turns his gaze back to me, a hand going up into my hair as he tilts my head back even more.

Placing a kiss on my forehead, he smiles down at me.

"I'm just happy to have you here…and sorry we had to go through all this just to get to this moment."

A rush of warmth comes across the bond as he leans forward and fuses his lips with mine, his tongue reaching for and stroking against mine in a sensual kiss.

I melt against him, a soft moan releasing from me, but even as we kiss, even as I feel that warmth coming through the bond, I can't help but think that there's something underneath it that I'm missing.

Something important.

And something that I need to fix.

23

Trudy

The Zarzenius is everything I didn't expect it to be.

The ship is golden and bigger than any transport I have ever seen before. Our shuttle looks like a bug approaching it.

"Oh my god…it's huge," I whisper.

Now dressed in one of his tunics, Qhenno has me seated in his lap in front of the view screen.

"It's Da'red's ship. Big enough to hold ten families."

My eyes widen. "Only ten? Pssh."

Qhenno chuckles and the sound of his laughter has me turning to watch the joy lift his features.

"Don't say that to Da'red. He might be the prince, but he hates when his family's importance is mentioned."

"That's kind of hard when you travel in a ship like that, isn't it?" I ask, my eyes widening a little as huge doors open on the Zarzenius to allow us to dock.

"This ship was the smallest one the crown had to offer."

My eyebrows lift and I shake my head.

Such wealth is only something that's dreamt about where I come from.

As our shuttle docks, the sound of the engine slowly dying, Qhenno waits until the lights blink off and we are sitting in the dim supplementary lights of the ship.

"Ready?" he asks.

I release a short breath and nod, wrapping my arms around his neck. I'm as ready as I'll ever be. "You said no one's on the ship?"

"Deserted. Aqnar is on Atar. And only the fates know where Da'red and Bhihan have gone," he replies, rising with me in his arms. As he crouches and exits the shuttle, the cooler air of the Zarzenius hits me with full force and I shiver a little.

"Then how did the ship open for us?"

As he walks steadily toward another set of doors, Qhenno grunts. "We joke that she's sentient sometimes," he replies.

At the furrow of my brow, he continues. "Zarzenius, adjust the temperature controls. A female is now on board."

"Scanning," the same voice I heard in the shuttle sounds on board this ship too. "Earthkin female present. Adjusting temperature controls."

Qhenno smiles again and steps through the large doors. Looking up at him now, I realize this is the most relaxed I've seen him since we met.

That male that was in the mines, the one whose eyes bled to black as he hunted down the male who had stolen from me and beat him to a pulp, that male is not here.

He's different right now.

Softer. More welcoming. Warmer.

And I realize he's always been that way with me. Not once has he ever shown me anything but care.

But despite that, as he steps into the ship and his shoulders sag from the strain of the last few days, there's still that shadow that lingers in his gaze. A shadow of something I missed.

"We're home, my ari," he says. "For now, at least. My real lodging is on Atar." He frowns a little. "I hope you will like it there."

I smile as he enters the ship, walking through a corridor filled with storage items before we enter a larger room.

It looks like a hotel in here. Like pictures on those holo boards that I used to see advertised. One of those same boards I fell off and had my accident.

God…that all seems like so long ago.

Glancing around as Qhenno walks, I don't realize he's looking at me until I lift my gaze to his.

"Like it?" he asks.

I nod. "Of course. It's…amazing."

"Good," he releases a breath, "because I do not know how long you will be stuck up here. I…did not expect to find my mate on this mission."

Moving my hand from his neck, I cup his jaw. "Qhenno…this is perfect."

There's a light in his eyes that twinkles a little. "Is it?"

I nod. "You've given me more than I could have ever imagined…"

"But if you could have chosen…"

I blink at him, my heart stuttering at the heaviness imbued in his words.

His throat moves as he stands before the outline of a door in the wall. After about a second's wait, it opens to reveal a pristine bedroom.

"My quarters," he says as he moves into the space and over to the bed. Leaning forward, he sets me down.

It feels like I'm lying on the softest feathers, but not even that can distract me from what I'm finally realizing.

"Oh my God…" I groan, reaching for him as he begins to move away.

Qhenno freezes, his eyes widening on me. "What's wrong?"

"Qhenno…" I breathe.

I can feel it now. The loneliness. The cold…*loneliness*. It's been there, lurking underneath the bond that binds us. But he hides it so well.

Staring at him now, my heart breaks.

"I've been so selfish," I whisper.

Qhenno looks at me, confused.

"I saw you as strong. Untouchable. *I* was the broken one."

He growls. "You are not broken."

"But I am," I say. "I was. In here." I touch my heart before moving my hand to his. "And you have been too."

I see the moment the walls go up. The pain that he hides so well disappearing behind the smile that he gives me.

"You do not have to worry about me," he says. "You are mine to—"

"But I do worry, because *you are mine too.*"

Qhenno gulps. It is the only indication I get that I might be on to the right thing after all.

"You said you searched for me for so long…your *mate.*"

His throat moves again, as if he has lost his voice…or maybe he's just unable to respond. Too afraid to go down the road where he's most vulnerable.

"You searched for me…and you found me…only for me to say I don't want a mate."

His throat moves again, some of the light leaving his eyes.

"And then I told you to mark me…" A lump forms in my throat. "Why do you think I told you to mark me?"

When he doesn't answer, my fears are realized.

"Oh, Qhenno." I pull him toward me and he doesn't resist. He collapses on top of me, the bed dipping slightly as I cradle his head to my breast. Tears well in my eyes. "Qhenno, I didn't say it, but I think you needed me to, didn't you?"

My mate doesn't answer, but he doesn't need to. I know exactly what he needs now.

"I want you. What we have now…what I feel for you…this bond… I've wanted it all my life. You have been out there waiting for me for so long, and I wish I'd known sooner. But we've found each other now." I bend and press a kiss to his forehead and Qhenno looks up at me. "I want this," I whisper, "maybe even more than you do."

Qhenno grins and surges upward, pinning me into the bed. "Impossible," he growls and I chuckle before forcing myself to sober.

"I need you to feel what I'm saying through this bond that binds us," I whisper, taking his hand to press against my heart. "Feel it. Feel that what I say is true. I only said I didn't want a mate because I was running away from pain I didn't want to feel. Truth is…I was lying."

Qhenno stares down at me and I can almost see that shadow, that uncertainty that was lingering disappear.

"No more lies," he whispers.

"No more lies."

"I want your fears and your pain. Your sorrow and your joy."

With that, he growls and suddenly dips his head, his lips closing over my neck as he grazes his fangs against the mark he made. I squeal and a growl rumbles in his throat.

"Again?" he asks.

"Again?" my eyes widen. We've already done it so many times that I'm sore and *still* that little bud between my folds stirs at his suggestion.

"I can smell your arousal, Trudy."

I squeal again. "Not fair!"

Qhenno chuckles.

"Already," he says, "you make me the happiest male that ever lived…and I intend to live my forever with you."

I warm, a smile I can't stop smooths my lips. "I want to spend my forever with you too."

Qhenno growls approval.

"But…there's something I have to ask you…"

At the seriousness of my tone, Qhenno stops nibbling on my neck and lifts his gaze to mine.

I clear my throat. I've been avoiding this conversation for so long.

"Anything, my ari."

"I will need to find a job in your world." My gaze darts to his. "I want to know that will be possible."

Qhenno growls. "After working so hard in the Morang mine, you want to work more?"

I huff a laugh through my nose. "Well, I need a way to support myself. They destroyed my chair early in this mess, and I need a new one."

"I enjoy carrying you in my arms," he growls almost petulantly and I chuckle.

"I appreciate you doing that, but I need to get around on my own, too."

Qhenno's brows furrow slightly. "I can procure a new transport device."

It's not what I expected him to say, but my brows rise anyway. "Transport device?"

"On your planet, you call it a wheeling chair?" he continues. "I can have an automated one delivered to my lodging. I was thinking of one of those newer models. The ones that transform into a standing device that will help you when I am not home."

Home. The thought makes me smile and I watch as Qhenno's gaze drifts off as he stares at nothing, listing off the different technology he's already thought of to help me transition to living with him.

He has already planned everything. Including me in every aspect of his life.

"I will have them remodel the washing room, so you will feel safer when taking baths, and the meal preparation room too," he continues, then pauses, his gaze finding mine. "Unless you want none of that. If you wish to have surgery instead, to fix your spine, I will pay for that too."

I open my mouth to answer, but all that happens is that I only blink at him.

"You would do all that for me?" I whisper.

Qhenno leans down, his lips brushing lightly against mine. "I want you to be comfortable. When I first saw you…saw how the Morang were treating you…" He growls, his nostrils flaring as his jaw ticks and I pull his head down to mine so I can brush my lips against his once more.

"Never again," he finally says. "I don't want you to feel that helpless ever again." He kisses me, his lips sliding over mine in the gentlest but most powerful kiss we've shared between us. "Whatever you need, my mate, I will provide."

My throat's gone dry and I know that if I think about his words, I will end up crying.

"But what about you? You want to give me all that…I don't have anything to give you. All I had is on Lower Earth and it's not much." I strangle a sad laugh. "It doesn't feel right…"

"What doesn't feel right?" Even as he speaks, I can feel his cock hardening once more and poking into my side. It makes it hard to focus.

"Taking everything you're willing to give and giving nothing back in return."

Qhenno tilts my head toward him, a frown marring his brow.

"My ari…" he begins. "You have no idea what you have given me, do you?"

His gaze searches mine before he continues. "My whole life, I have wanted a mate. You. I have wanted *you*. Begged the fates for you. Pleaded for you. *Craved* you. And now, I finally have you. You are the greatest gift I have wanted all my life. I would give away everything I have earned thus far, if I can only have you in return."

Moving his thumb to my cheek, his gaze softens as he looks down at me.

"You have healed a part of me I didn't know needed healing until I held you in my arms. Trudy…"

"Yes?" I whisper.

"You are the reason I breathe. I will do everything in my power to make you happy."

I grip his arm, the one that's grasping my chin, and I pull it to my jaw, tilting my head in his embrace.

"If you do not like the plans I have made about your mobility chair, we can always change them," he continues.

I laugh. A genuine one filled with relief and happiness. "No…your plan sounds great."

Qhenno pauses, a soft smile on his lips as he uses his nose to brush against mine.

"My ari…" he groans, his cock growing even harder against me.

"Yes…"

"You are mine," he growls and my body responds immediately.

"I am yours…"

And I can't believe he is mine.

EPILOGUE

Qhenno

I'm still waiting to hear if there's any fallout from the Morang, but it seems the whole cohort that had been operating that mine is dead.

Good.

As the days pass, any worry I had concerning those scum slowly dies to be replaced by a whole other worry instead.

Bhihan is still nowhere to be seen.

It has been several cycles with no word from him.

"Do you think he's okay?" Trudy asks, the hum of her motorized *wheelchair*, as she calls it, only slightly audible as she drives onto the bridge.

Delivery was quick, considering we are not hovering over a planet.

"How did you know I am thinking about him?" I ask, turning away from the schematics that are tracking the location of not only Bhihan, but the crown prince as well.

"You get this sort of snarl on your face that I've only seen when you're thinking about him."

"He can be an idiot sometimes. Don't let him know this when he returns, but it makes me worry."

Trudy laughs and moves her chair over to me. As I lean down to capture her lips in mine, the swipe of her tongue makes me groan.

"You'll be a good father, someday," she says.

I try not to react to those words. To not let her know how much it affects me, but the growing color in her cheeks lets me know she already knows exactly what I am feeling.

The bond.

I can't hide anything from my mate...and...well...I don't want to.

"It's not something I have ever really thought about until you..." she whispers onto my lips.

"I want whatever you want," I reply.

"Liar," she chuckles before running her tongue down my lip. "You want a baby. A soft little thing that looks just like me."

My fangs extend at her words and she swipes her tongue across one, a fist tugging into my tunic as she pulls me closer.

"How did you know that?" I can't help the need that deepens my voice. I want everything she just said so badly that my cock is already hard and filled with seed to do the job.

"Every time we make love and you think I'm asleep, you hold my belly and whisper those words." Trudy looks into my eyes, a twinkle in hers.

I clear the lump from my throat. "I didn't know you were awake."

"I know, and that's why I found it so sweet."

Slight embarrassment makes me want to change the subject, yet, the fact she's known this all along makes my cock throb even harder.

"How long will we be alone?" she whispers.

"There's no telling when the others will return." My voice is so hoarse, my Galactic Standard sounds more like Uulvian.

Trudy gives me a look I have never seen her give me before. Her eyes twinkle and she licks her lips as she pulls me in even closer. The darkness, that heaviness that was present no longer shadows her face. She is happier now and her happiness warms me...and hardens my cock.

"Qef..." I breathe as it presses into my trou.

"Maybe we should make use of the time..." she whispers.

"Maybe…try to fill my belly with as much seed as you can…you know…improve the chances."

My cock jerks, pre-spend soaking my trou at the thought.

"How long do you think it will take?" she whispers against my lips, nipping the corner of mine and eliciting a growl from my throat.

"Trudy…" I warn.

"How many times do you think you can fill me up before I can't be filled anymore…?"

"Trudy…" I warn again, my voice growing sterner, but I cannot resist the pull of this female. She draws me like a magnet and my growl is lost in her mouth as she captures my lips.

"Take me to your quarters, my ari," she whispers.

Another growl leaves my throat, my insides going to jelly with the Atari term she used.

"I don't deserve you," I whisper, lifting her from her chair and hurrying from the bridge, stripping my trou as I walk.

"No, Qhenno…" Trudy whispers, her hand clasping my jaw, and she looks deep into my eyes. "*I don't deserve you.*"

As I collapse on the bed and sink into my mate over and over again, Trudy whimpers my name. And then she whimpers something else. Something she has never said to me before.

"I love you, Qhenno. So so much. I love you so much."

My heart swells a thousand times its size as I hold her close and bury myself deep inside her, streams of my spend filling her tight little pussy and marking her even more as mine.

"I love you too, my ari.

…

You are the reason I breathe."

AFTERWORD

♥ This concludes Claiming His Mate. ♥

When I first wrote this book, I submitted it to the Claimed Among the Stars Anthology. At first, it was simply a fun project. I did not anticipate that Marion and Aqnar's story would find its way into so many of your hearts!

This extended version was created with lots of love.

I found myself quite admiring Marion. Her fears felt so real, almost as if she were my friend and she was speaking to me. And Aqnar...I felt his pain at the end there. I desperately wanted them to find their way back to each other. (I know it may sound strange since, I am the one writing it, :D. But, while the words come out on paper, I feel every single one of them.)

This is much lighter than my last series—Captured Earth, where the villains really give you a reason to shiver and hide underneath your blanket. If you are looking for something dark and a bit terrifying, you should read that :D.

Thank you so much for reading and as always, lots of love and many blessings!

♥ A.G.

Scan the QR code below if you want to ☞ Join my mailing list, ☞ Find me on Facebook , or ☞ Join my Patreon (exclusive access NSFW character art, ARCs, quarterly mailouts and more!)

Craving His Mate

From the moment my fangs began to drip with life spirit, I have known I wanted a mate. One to love. One to care for. *A female all for myself.*

But as the moons pass by, the fates have denied me.

Until I see her.

She is different. She is human. *And she is vulnerable.* More vulnerable than I could have ever imagined.

But she is *mine*. Mine to cherish, mine to keep, and I will do everything in my power to let her know that the moment I laid my eyes on her, she became the reason I breathe.

ALSO BY AGWILDE

Xul: Captured by Aliens Book One
Athena wakes up in hell.
Well…it's an alien slave ship, but it might as well be hell because she only has three choices.
Mate. Become a sex slave. Or be killed.
Great options.

Desperate for freedom, a chance for survival is presented in the handsome rogue alien called Xul.

But Xul is caught up in problems of his own and a mission he cannot afford to let fail—one that could be easily compromised if he dared open his heart.

That doesn't leave her with many options and it doesn't help that she finds him utterly frustrating...

...and strong, hot, irresistible…

She shouldn't really be thinking about him like that. Should she?

Other books in the series: Crex, Yce, Kyris, Kyro

——

Riv's Sanctuary: Riv's Sanctuary Book One

Abducted from Earth over a year ago, Lauren spent most of that time getting accustomed to her new life as one of the "animals" in an alien zoo.

When she's sold by the zookeeper, her life takes a turn she wasn't expecting. She has no idea where she'll end up till she's brought to a sanctuary owned by a tall blue hunk of an alien called Riv.

Riv's life is quiet and peaceful in a place as far away from civilization as he can manage. So when an annoying chatterbox of a human ends up on his doorstep, he's less than pleased. The human disrupts his life and his solitude and he can't wait to get rid of her.

He's not interested in helping her, and he's definitely not interested in love.

Except…she's managed to wheedle her way in and suddenly those barriers around his heart don't seem so strong anymore.

He has two options: Let her go.

Or let her in.

Other books in the series: Sohut's Protection, Ka'Cit's Haven

——

Ajos: The Restitution Book One

She didn't move to the big city just to be kidnapped by aliens.

That wasn't even possible...

Right?

WRONG.

When Kerena wakes up, she's not on Earth anymore.

Heck, she's not even in the same galaxy, and the face hovering so close she can make out every detail? That face is definitely...not...human.

But before she can really figure out what's going on, Kerena realizes she's caught in the middle of a war—one she was thrust into as soon as she was ripped from Earth.

She's surrounded by aliens in a rebellion, but there's one—the one with the strange golden eyes, minty-teal skin, and rippling muscles—that holds her attention.

His presence is magnetic and his heated gaze makes something stir deep within her.

He's battling something that has nothing to do with the war and his warning that she should stay away does not go unheeded.

He's a dangerous rebel fighter. She gets that. So...why is he still hovering so close? And why is he growling at everyone that so much as looks in her direction?

Most of all, why does he keep looking at her like she belongs to ... HIM?

———

Arrival: Captured Earth Book One

ADIRA

The machines came, and they trampled us all.

I have nothing left. No family. No friends. No home.

They harvest us. They breed us. They feed from us…

There is no hope…Not until one fateful moment when my eyes open and I see something streaking across the skies.

What appears is like a demon before my eyes…

But can they be worse than the evil already upon us?

I will just have to wait and see.

FER'RO

Sailing across the stars for what feels like eons…we have followed our enemy to a little blue planet.

We had wanted to arrive before them…now I think we may be too late.
But when we kill the first Scrit and I see the being drowning within its depths, I know I have to save it.
And *it*…turns out to be a *her*. **A female.**
This planet has hope yet. I will save her and her kind.
…Little do I know…she's the one who ends up saving me instead.

Dark. Steamy. Gritty. A thrilling romance intertwined in a plot that will give you chills.

Other books in the series: Base Zero, Cataclysm, War

———

Scan the QR code to view all books

ABOUT THE AUTHOR

A. G. Wilde is an avid reader, a gamer, a lover of all things space, alien, and sci-fi.

She is addicted to intense romance, irresistible heroes, and deliciously naughty things.

❀☆☼☆❀

patreon.com/agwilde
facebook.com/agwilde
twitter.com/authoragwilde
instagram.com/authoragwilde
amazon.com/author/agwilde